JOURNEY UNDER THE ARCTIC

Also in the
Fabien Cousteau Expeditions

GREAT WHITE SHARK ADVENTURE

FABIEN COUSTEAU EXPEDITIONS

JOURNEY UNDER THE ARCTIC

WRITTEN BY
JAMES O. FRAIOLI

ILLUSTRATED BY
JOE ST.PIERRE

MARGARET K. McELDERRY BOOKS
NEW YORK LONDON TORONTO SYDNEY NEW DELHI

AUTHORS' NOTE

Journey under the Arctic is a work of fiction
based on actual expeditions and accepted ideas
about the Arctic and its inhabitants.

MARGARET K. McELDERRY BOOKS
An imprint of Simon & Schuster Children's Publishing Division
1230 Avenue of the Americas, New York, New York 10020
Text copyright © 2020 by James O. Fraioli and Fabien Cousteau
Illustrations copyright © 2020 by Joseph St.Pierre
MARGARET K. McELDERRY BOOKS is a trademark of Simon & Schuster, Inc.
For information about special discounts for bulk purchases, please contact Simon & Schuster
Special Sales at 1-866-506-1949 or business@simonandschuster.com.
The Simon & Schuster Speakers Bureau can bring authors to your live event.
For more information or to book an event, contact the Simon & Schuster Speakers
Bureau at 1-866-248-3049 or visit our website at www.simonspeakers.com.
Also available in a Margaret K. McElderry Books hardcover edition
Book design by Sonia Chaghatzbanian
The text for this book was set in Wild and Crazy.
The illustrations for this book were rendered digitally.
Manufactured in China
1219 SCP
First Margaret K. McElderry Books paper-over-board edition March 2020
10 9 8 7 6 5 4 3 2 1
Library of Congress Cataloging-in-Publication Data
Names: Fraioli, James O., 1968– author. | St. Pierre, Joe, illustrator. | Cousteau, Fabien.
Title: Journey under the Arctic / written by James O. Fraioli ; illustrated by Joe St. Pierre.
Description: First edition. | New York, New York : Margaret K. McElderry Books, [2020] | Series:
[Fabien Cousteau expeditions ; 2] | Audience: Ages 8–12. | Audience: Grades 4–6. | Summary:
Junior explorers Rocco and Olivia join Fabien Cousteau and his research team on an icebreaker
in the Arctic Circle, seeking the rare dumbo octopus. Inserts include facts about the effects of
climate change, people and animals of the Arctic, and ships that have explored the area.
Identifiers: LCCN 2019041176 (print) | ISBN 9781534420908 (paper-over-board) |
ISBN 9781534420915 (hardcover) | ISBN 9781534420922 (eBook)
Subjects: LCSH: Graphic novels. | CYAC: Graphic novels. | Octopuses—Fiction. | Rare
animals—Fiction. | Cousteau, Fabien, Fiction. | Scientists—Fiction. | Arctic regions—Fiction.
Classification: LCC PZ7.7.F72 Jou 2020 (print) | DDC [Fic]—dc23
LC record available at https://lccn.loc.gov/2019041176

JOURNEY UNDER THE ARCTIC

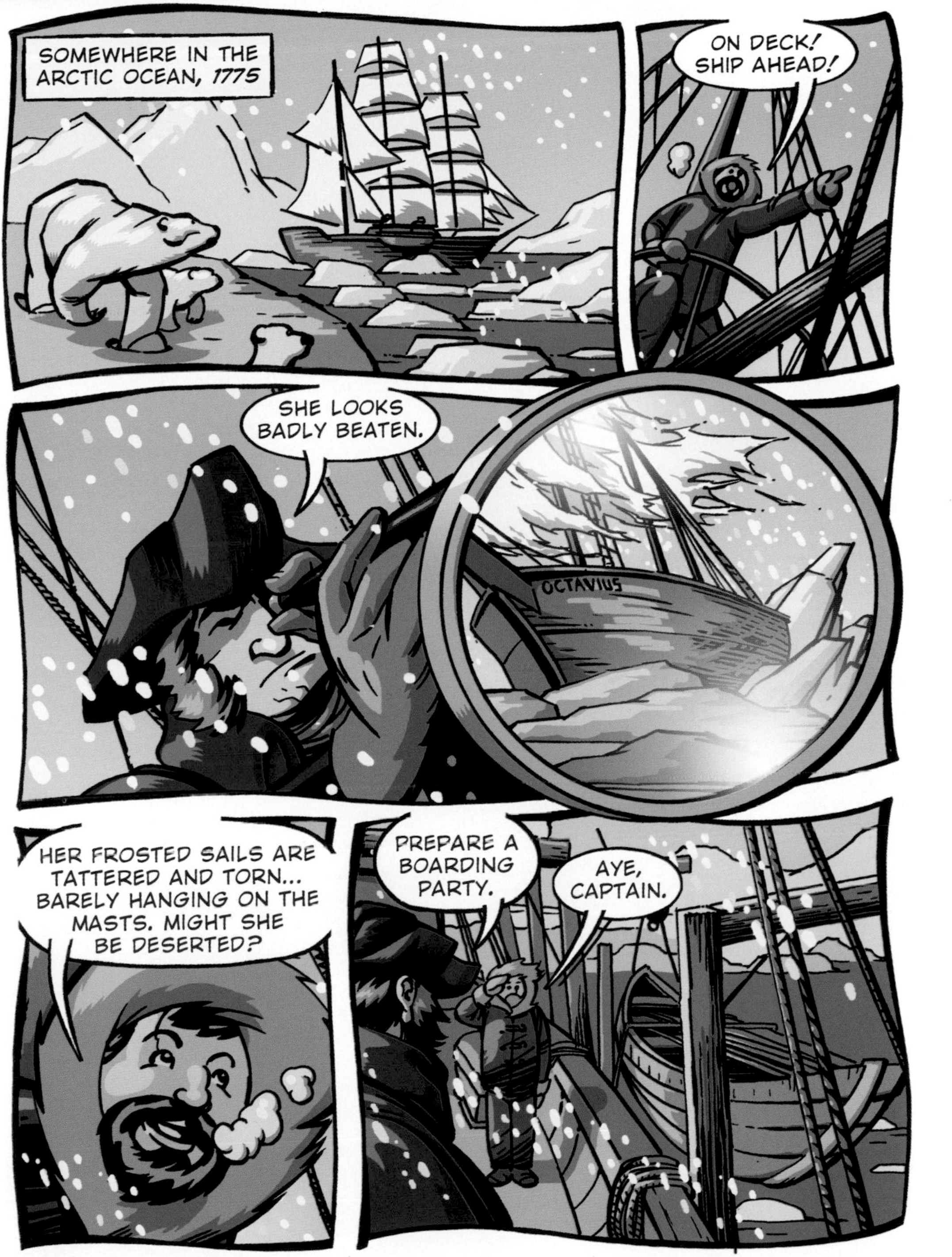
SOMEWHERE IN THE ARCTIC OCEAN, 1775
ON DECK! SHIP AHEAD!
SHE LOOKS BADLY BEATEN.
OCTAVIUS
HER FROSTED SAILS ARE TATTERED AND TORN... BARELY HANGING ON THE MASTS. MIGHT SHE BE DESERTED?
PREPARE A BOARDING PARTY.
AYE, CAPTAIN.

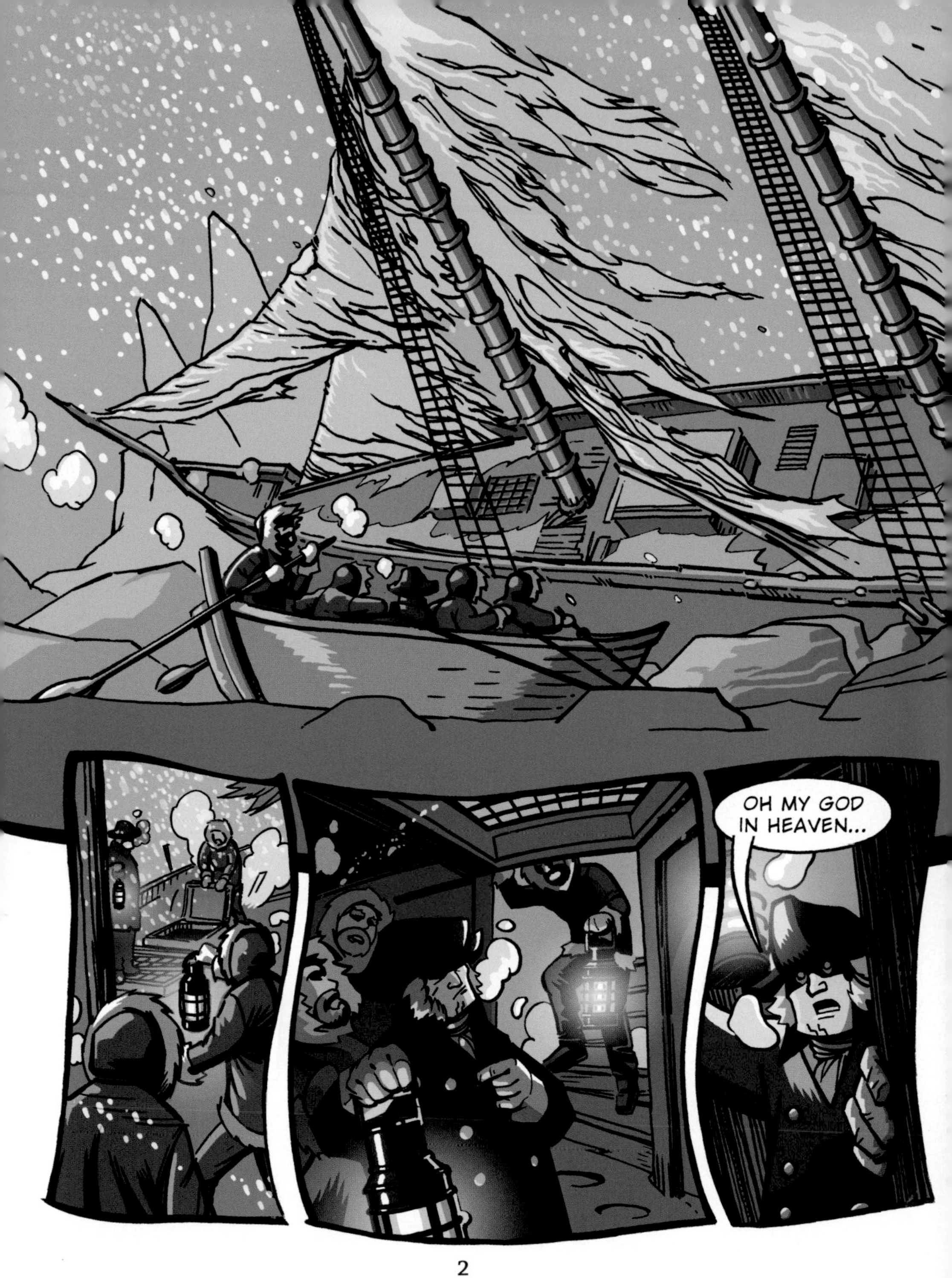
OH MY GOD IN HEAVEN...

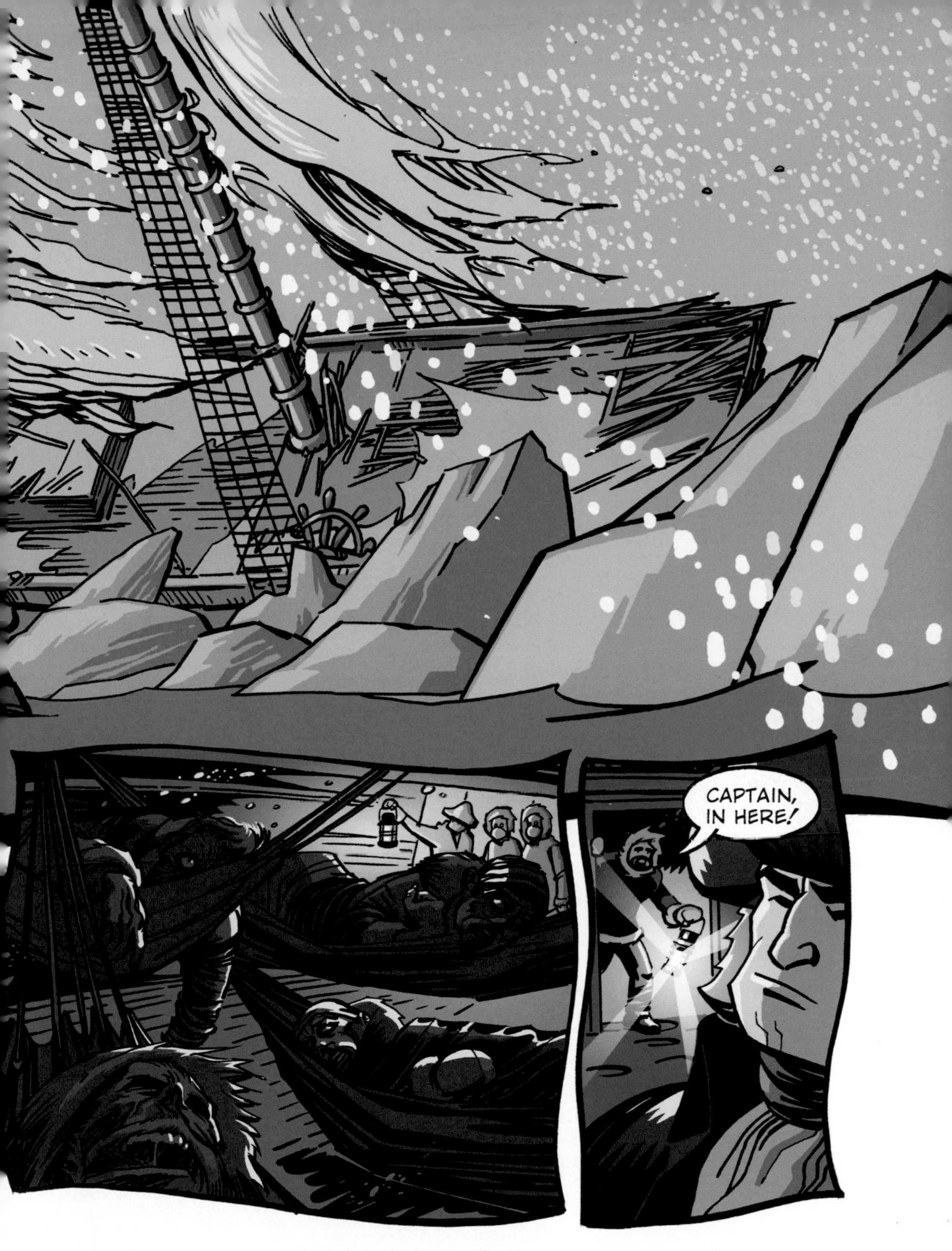
CAPTAIN, IN HERE!

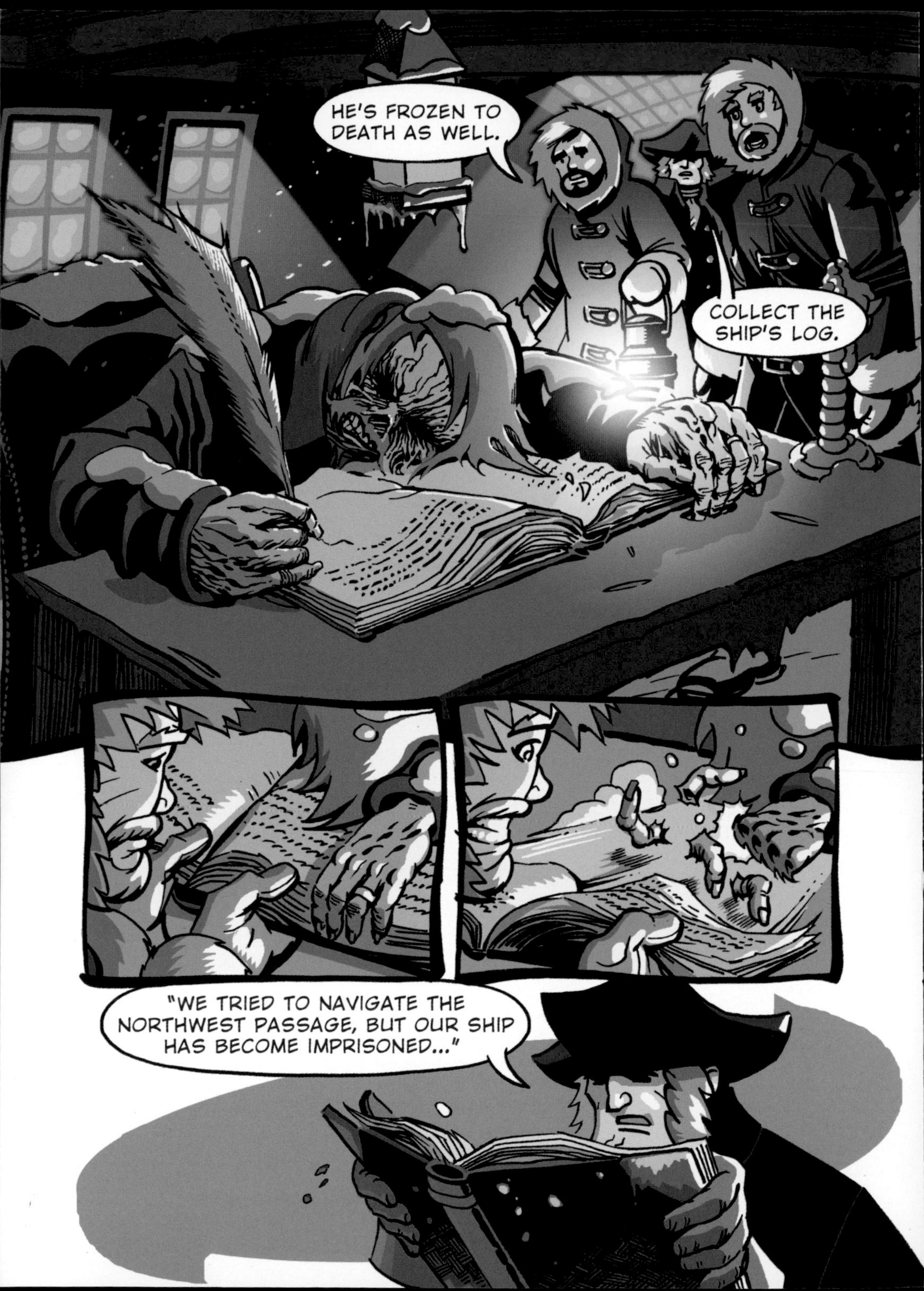
HE'S FROZEN TO DEATH AS WELL.
COLLECT THE SHIP'S LOG.
"WE TRIED TO NAVIGATE THE NORTHWEST PASSAGE, BUT OUR SHIP HAS BECOME IMPRISONED..."

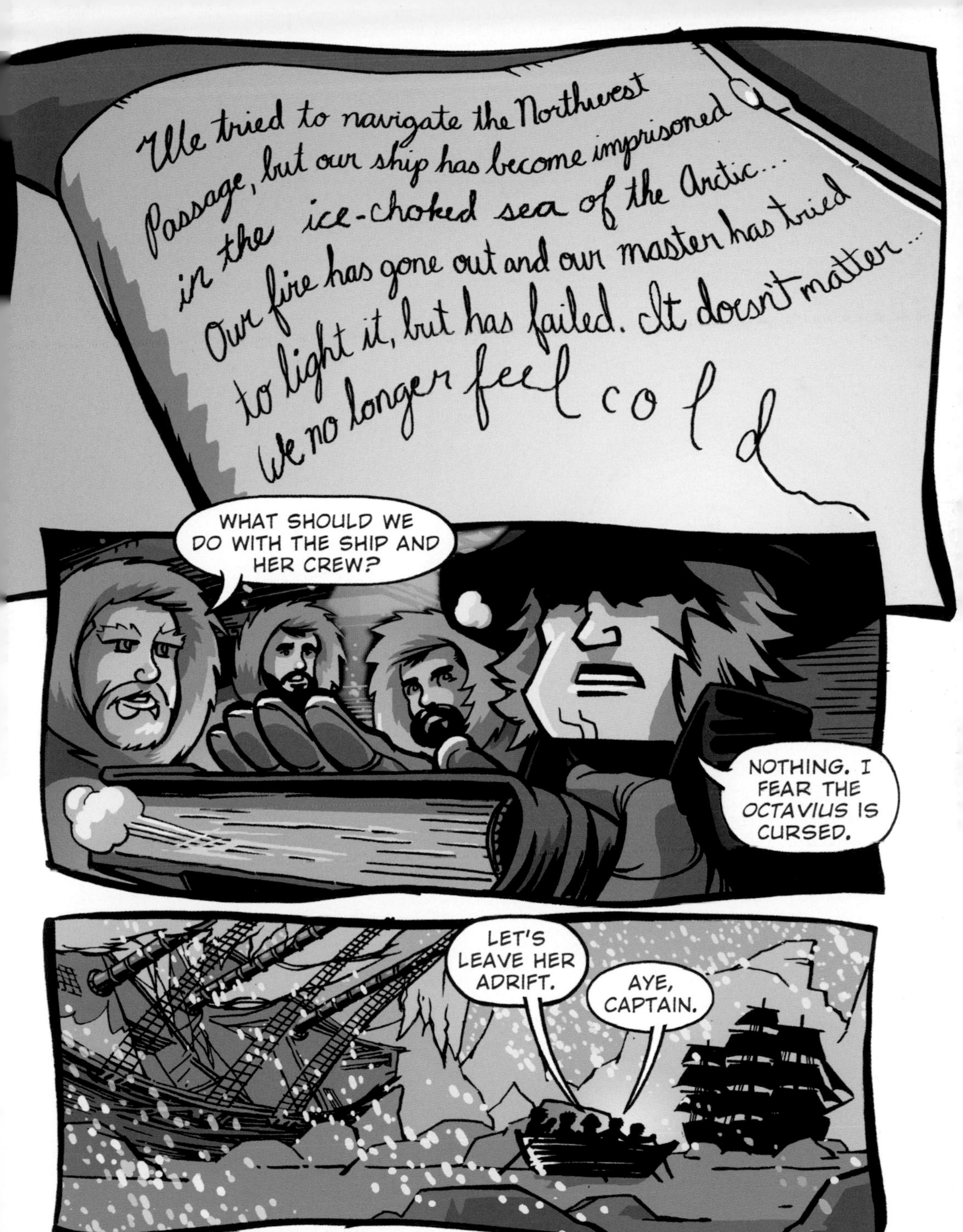
We tried to navigate the Northwest Passage, but our ship has become imprisoned in the ice-choked sea of the Arctic... Our fire has gone out and our master has tried to light it, but has failed. It doesn't matter... We no longer feel cold
WHAT SHOULD WE DO WITH THE SHIP AND HER CREW?
NOTHING. I FEAR THE *OCTAVIUS* IS CURSED.
LET'S LEAVE HER ADRIFT.
AYE, CAPTAIN.

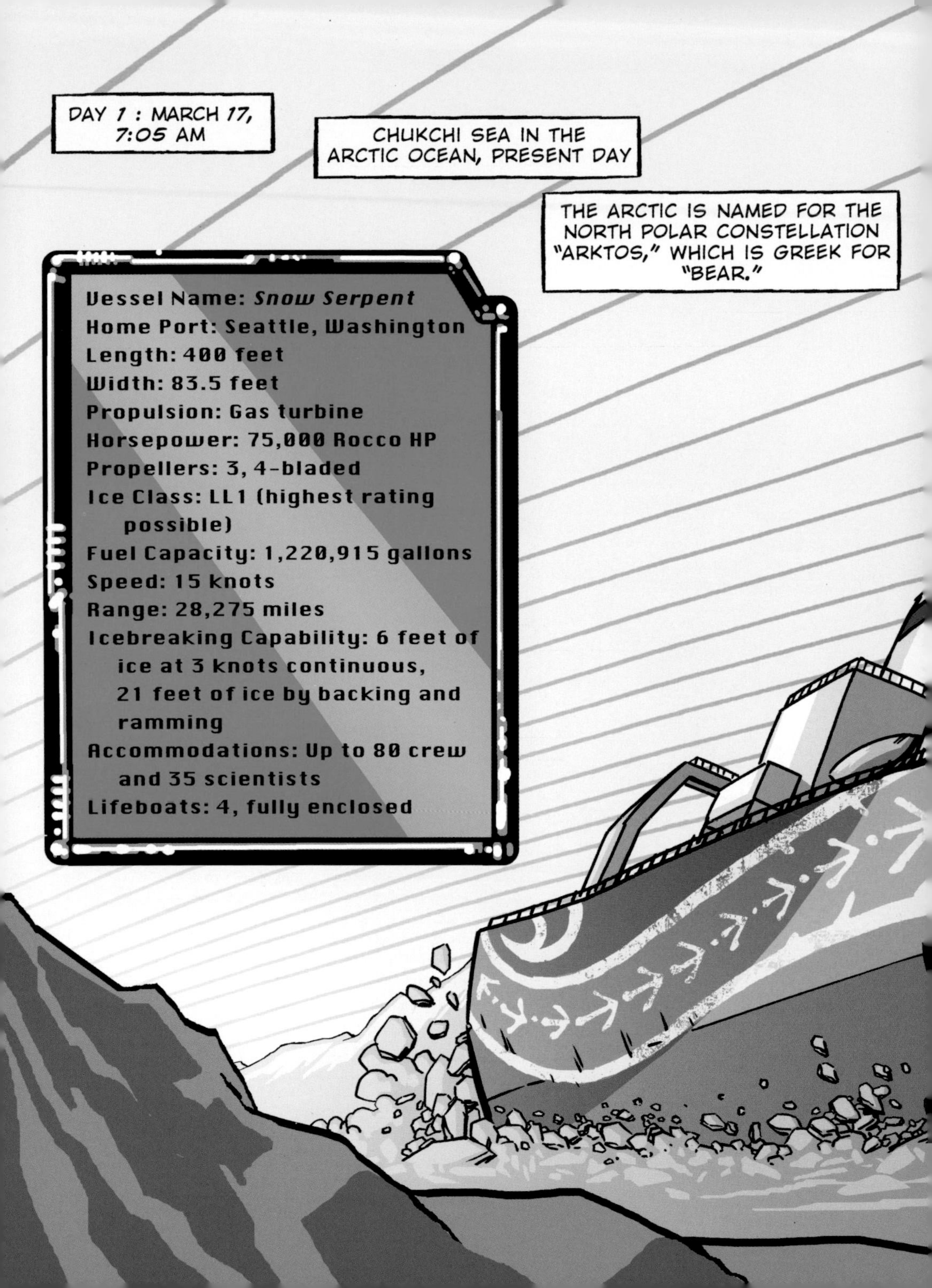
DAY 1 : MARCH 17, 7:05 AM
CHUKCHI SEA IN THE ARCTIC OCEAN, PRESENT DAY
THE ARCTIC IS NAMED FOR THE NORTH POLAR CONSTELLATION "ARKTOS," WHICH IS GREEK FOR "BEAR."
Vessel Name: *Snow Serpent*
Home Port: Seattle, Washington
Length: 400 feet
Width: 83.5 feet
Propulsion: Gas turbine
Horsepower: 75,000 Rocco HP
Propellers: 3, 4-bladed
Ice Class: LL1 (highest rating possible)
Fuel Capacity: 1,220,915 gallons
Speed: 15 knots
Range: 28,275 miles
Icebreaking Capability: 6 feet of ice at 3 knots continuous, 21 feet of ice by backing and ramming
Accommodations: Up to 80 crew and 35 scientists
Lifeboats: 4, fully enclosed

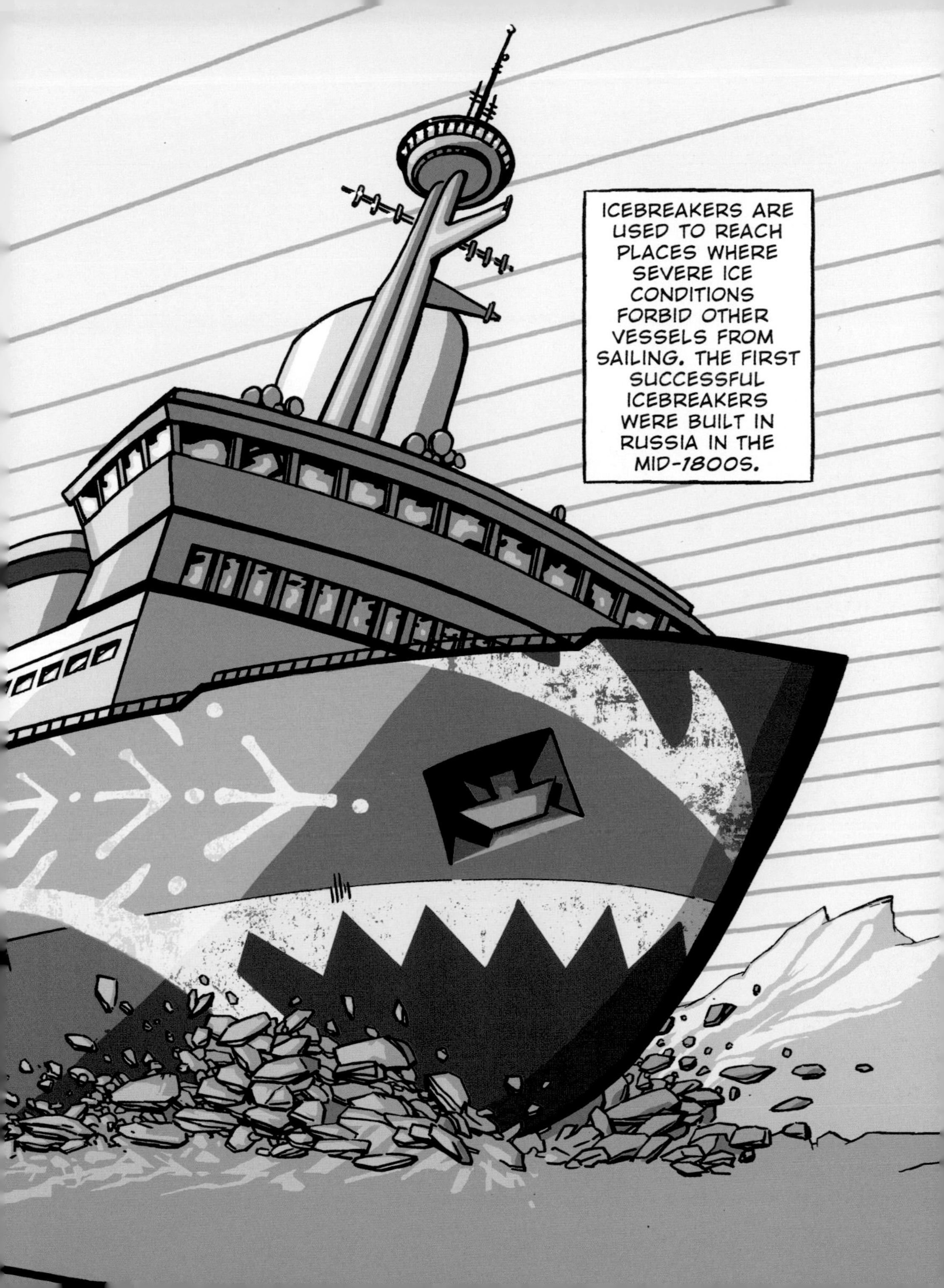
ICEBREAKERS ARE USED TO REACH PLACES WHERE SEVERE ICE CONDITIONS FORBID OTHER VESSELS FROM SAILING. THE FIRST SUCCESSFUL ICEBREAKERS WERE BUILT IN RUSSIA IN THE MID-1800S.

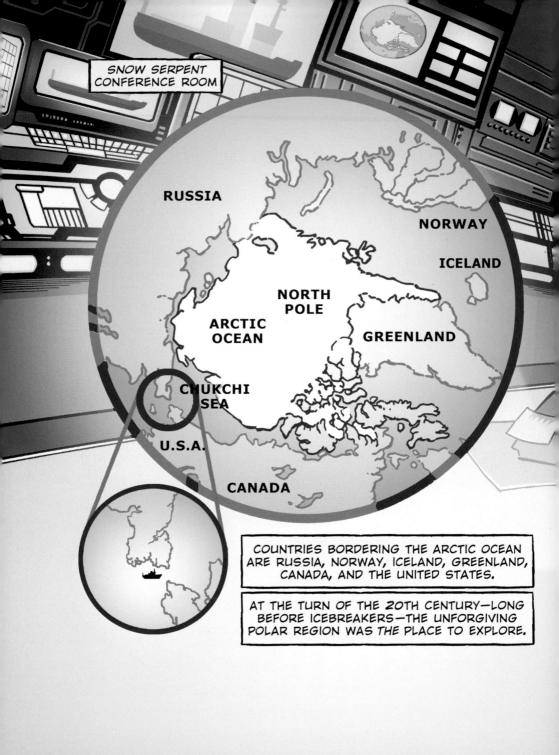

SNOW SERPENT
CONFERENCE ROOM

RUSSIA

NORWAY

ICELAND

NORTH
POLE

ARCTIC
OCEAN

GREENLAND

CHUKCHI
SEA

U.S.A.

CANADA

COUNTRIES BORDERING THE ARCTIC OCEAN
ARE RUSSIA, NORWAY, ICELAND, GREENLAND,
CANADA, AND THE UNITED STATES.

AT THE TURN OF THE 20TH CENTURY—LONG
BEFORE ICEBREAKERS—THE UNFORGIVING
POLAR REGION WAS THE PLACE TO EXPLORE.

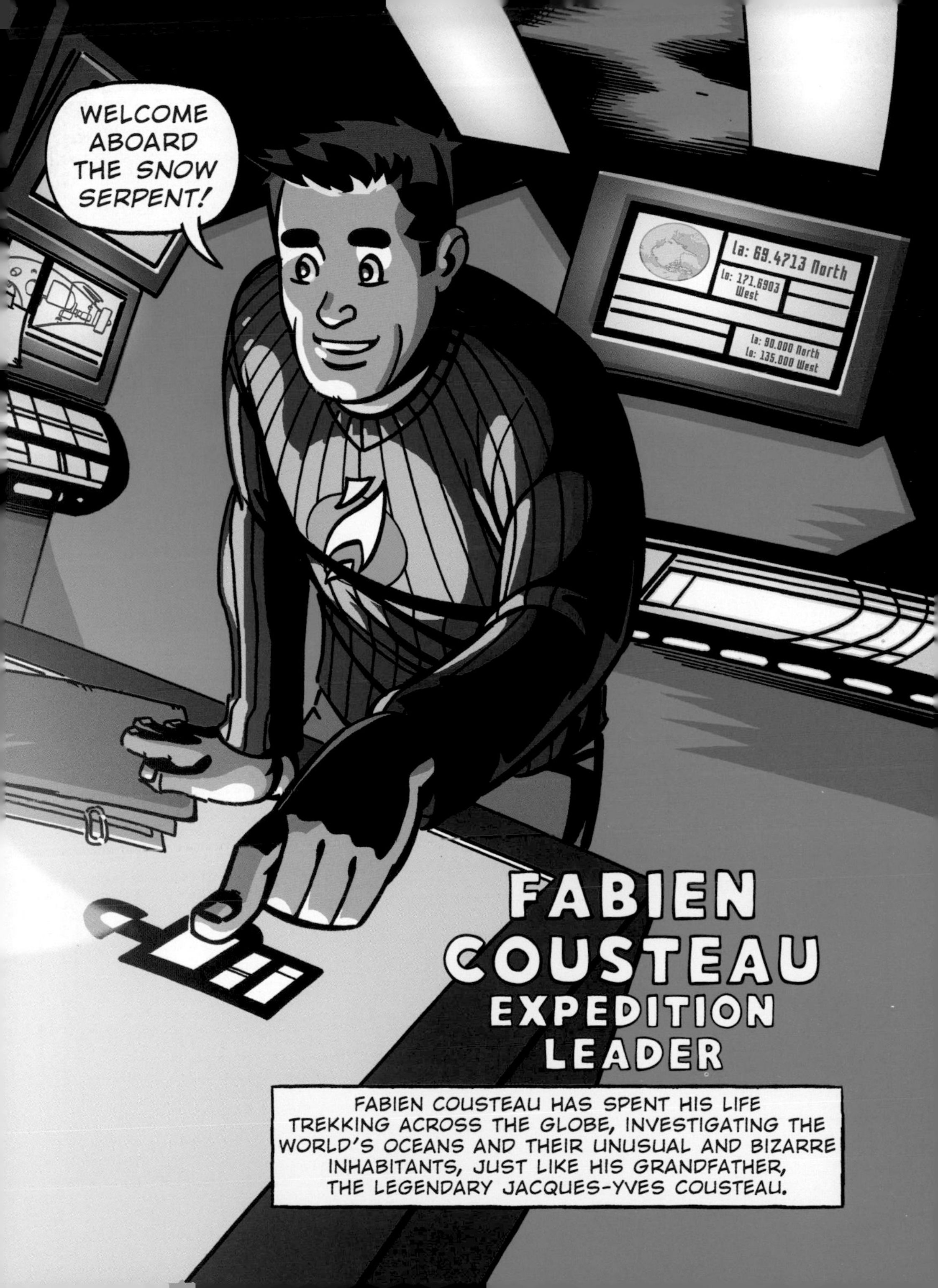
WELCOME ABOARD THE SNOW SERPENT!
la: 69.4713 North
lo: 171.6903 West
la: 90.000 North
lo: 135.000 West
FABIEN COUSTEAU
EXPEDITION LEADER
FABIEN COUSTEAU HAS SPENT HIS LIFE TREKKING ACROSS THE GLOBE, INVESTIGATING THE WORLD'S OCEANS AND THEIR UNUSUAL AND BIZARRE INHABITANTS, JUST LIKE HIS GRANDFATHER, THE LEGENDARY JACQUES-YVES COUSTEAU.

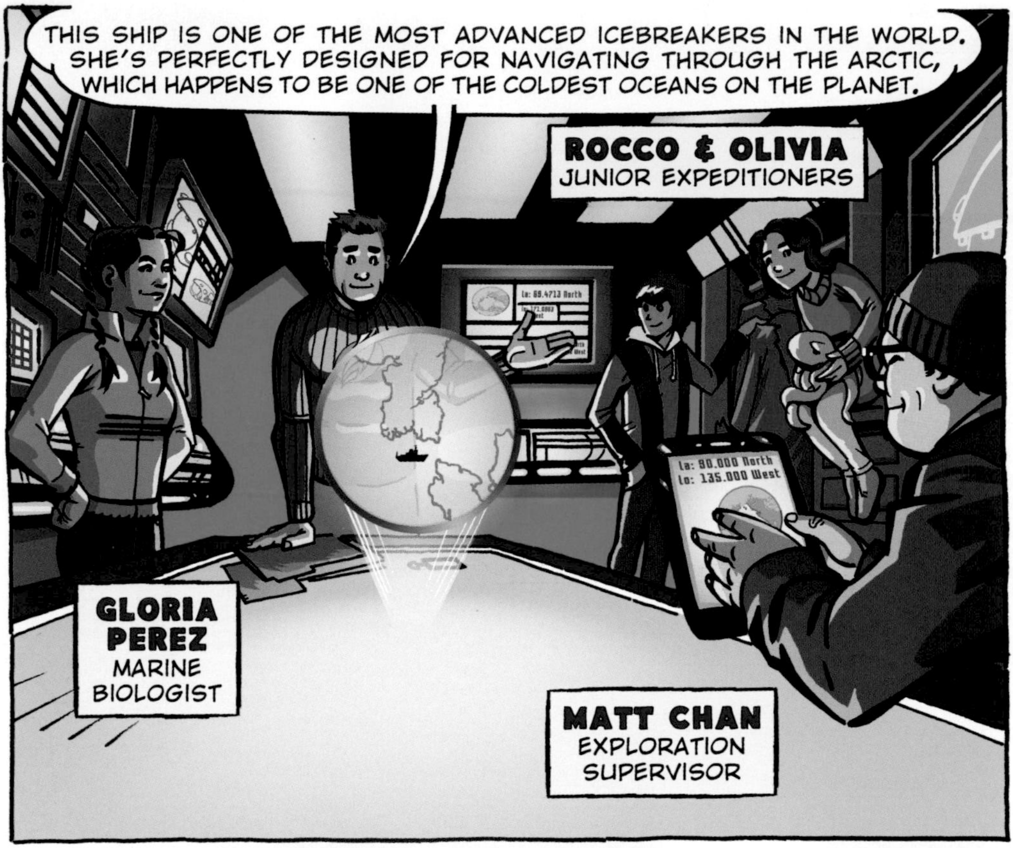
THIS SHIP IS ONE OF THE MOST ADVANCED ICEBREAKERS IN THE WORLD. SHE'S PERFECTLY DESIGNED FOR NAVIGATING THROUGH THE ARCTIC, WHICH HAPPENS TO BE ONE OF THE COLDEST OCEANS ON THE PLANET.
ROCCO & OLIVIA JUNIOR EXPEDITIONERS
la: 90.000 North
lo: 135.000 West
GLORIA PEREZ MARINE BIOLOGIST
MATT CHAN EXPLORATION SUPERVISOR

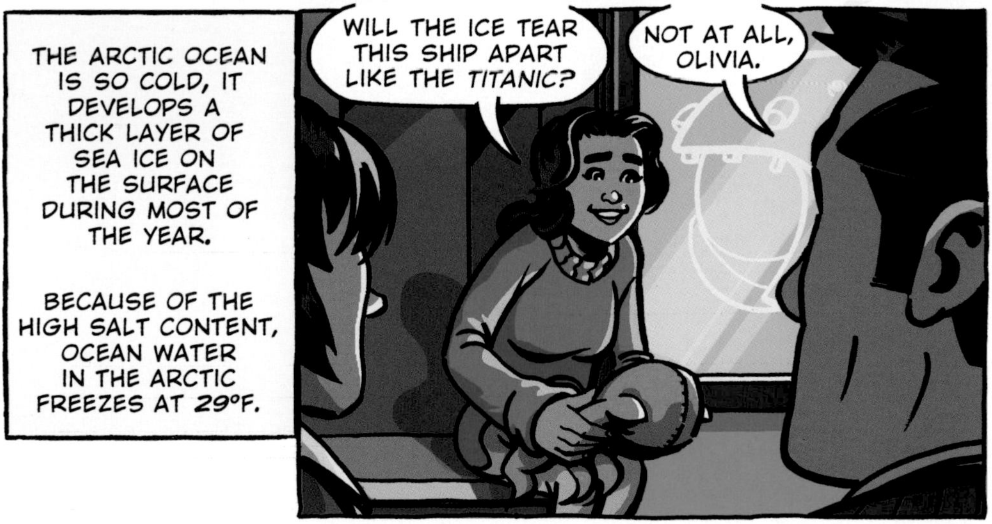
THE ARCTIC OCEAN IS SO COLD, IT DEVELOPS A THICK LAYER OF SEA ICE ON THE SURFACE DURING MOST OF THE YEAR.
BECAUSE OF THE HIGH SALT CONTENT, OCEAN WATER IN THE ARCTIC FREEZES AT 29°F.
WILL THE ICE TEAR THIS SHIP APART LIKE THE *TITANIC*?
NOT AT ALL, OLIVIA.

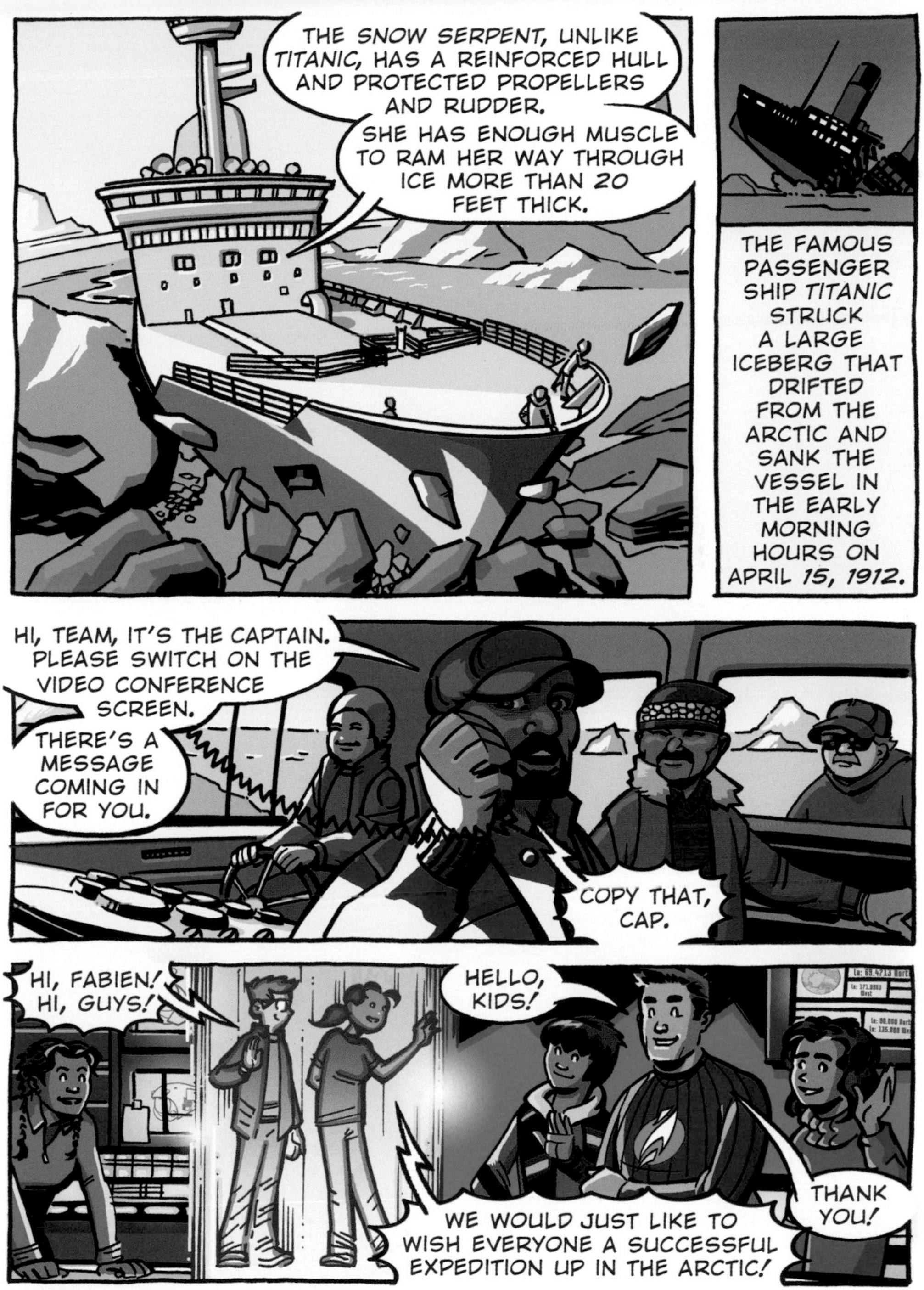
THE *SNOW SERPENT*, UNLIKE *TITANIC*, HAS A REINFORCED HULL AND PROTECTED PROPELLERS AND RUDDER.
SHE HAS ENOUGH MUSCLE TO RAM HER WAY THROUGH ICE MORE THAN 20 FEET THICK.
THE FAMOUS PASSENGER SHIP *TITANIC* STRUCK A LARGE ICEBERG THAT DRIFTED FROM THE ARCTIC AND SANK THE VESSEL IN THE EARLY MORNING HOURS ON APRIL 15, 1912.
HI, TEAM, IT'S THE CAPTAIN. PLEASE SWITCH ON THE VIDEO CONFERENCE SCREEN.
THERE'S A MESSAGE COMING IN FOR YOU.
COPY THAT, CAP.
HI, FABIEN! HI, GUYS!
HELLO, KIDS!
WE WOULD JUST LIKE TO WISH EVERYONE A SUCCESSFUL EXPEDITION UP IN THE ARCTIC!
THANK YOU!

WE WOULD ALSO LIKE TO LET YOU KNOW THAT BELLA, THE MONSTER SHARK WE TAGGED IN SOUTH AFRICA, IS DOING GREAT AND MIGRATING A LONG DISTANCE. SHE WAS LAST SPOTTED OFF THE NEPTUNE ISLANDS IN SOUTH AUSTRALIA.

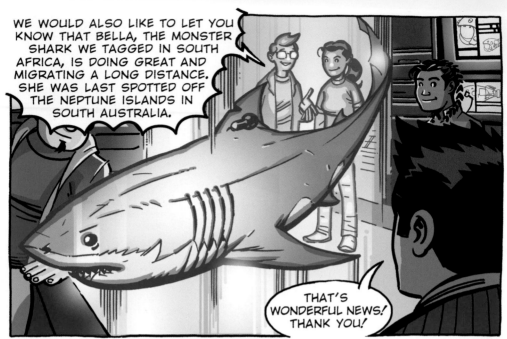

THAT'S WONDERFUL NEWS! THANK YOU!

BE SAFE UP THERE, AND WE'LL TALK TO YOU SOON!

WILL DO. THANKS, KIDS!

SORRY TO INTERRUPT, BUT ALL OF YOU BETTER HOLD ON. I'M ABOUT TO INCREASE THE SPEED SO MOST OF THE BROKEN ICE FRAGMENTS CAN BE PUSHED AWAY FROM THE PROPELLERS.

THE LARGEST KNOWN ICEBERG, REPORTED BY A UNITED STATES COAST GUARD ICEBREAKER IN *1957*, MEASURED MORE THAN *550* FEET TALL, ABOUT THE SAME HEIGHT AS A *55*-STORY BUILDING.

SOON WE WILL BE ON TOP OF THE WORLD AND THOUSANDS OF FEET BENEATH THE ARCTIC OCEAN.
I'M SO EXCITED!
ME TOO!
YOU MIGHT THINK THESE ICY WATERS ARE VOID OF LIFE BUT, IN REALITY, A RICH ECOSYSTEM FLOURISHES BELOW...
WHICH BRINGS US TO OUR MISSION: TO FIND A DUMBO OCTOPUS, ONE OF THE RAREST OCTOPI ON EARTH!
I'VE BEEN STUDYING OCTOPI AROUND THE GLOBE, BUT I'VE NEVER SEEN A DUMBO OCTOPUS!
WHAT MAKES THE DUMBO OCTOPUS SO SPECIAL?
GREAT QUESTION, ROCCO. BECAUSE THESE AMAZING CREATURES HAVE LEARNED TO SURVIVE IN SUCH COLD, DARK, AND HOSTILE PLACES, LIKE THE ARCTIC, WE'RE HOPING THEY MAY ONE DAY HELP US TO ADAPT AND SURVIVE IN SIMILAR ENVIRONMENTS.

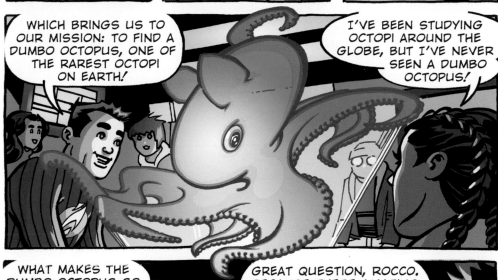

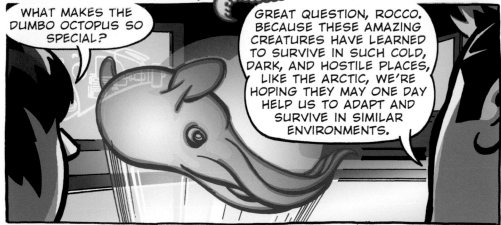

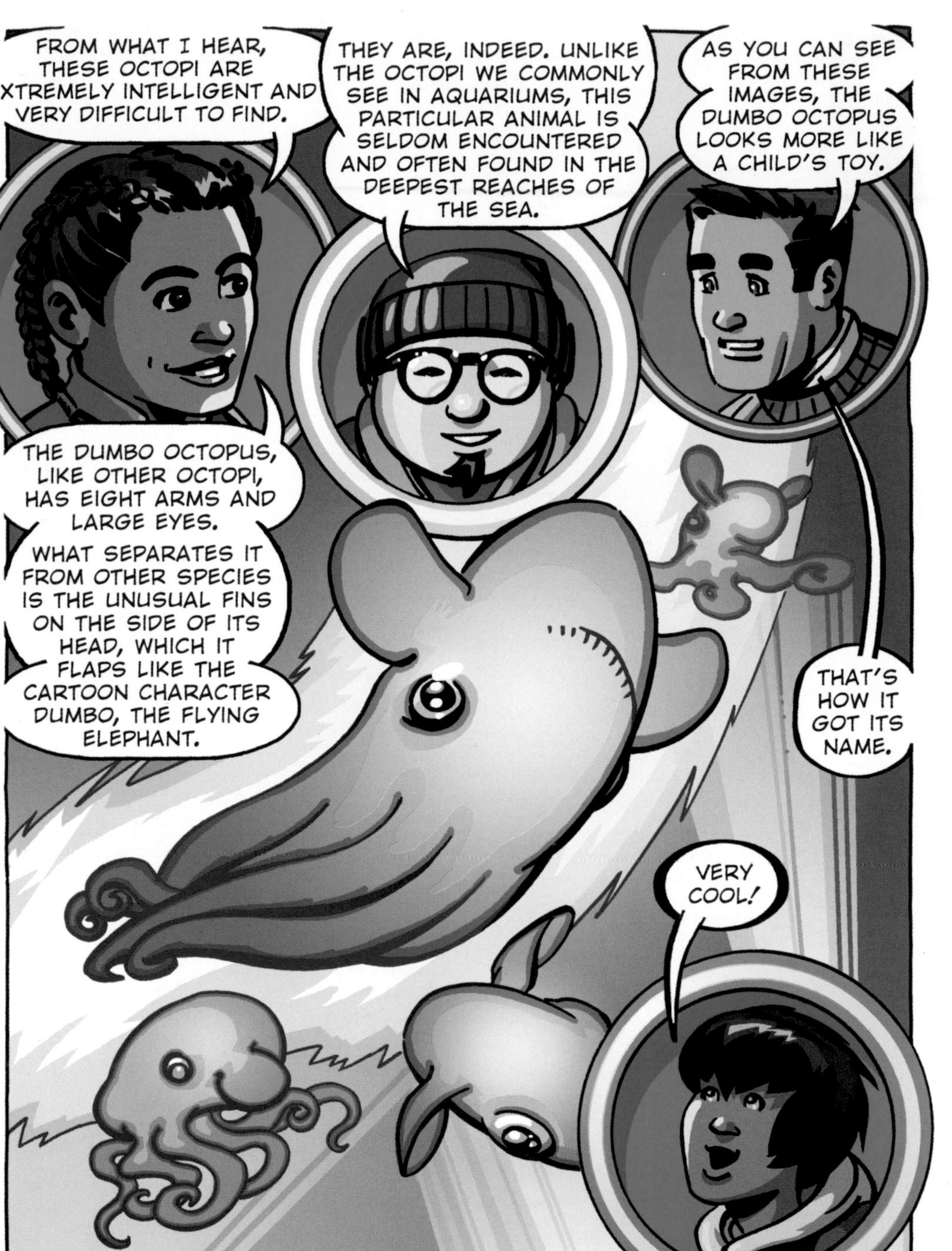
FROM WHAT I HEAR, THESE OCTOPI ARE EXTREMELY INTELLIGENT AND VERY DIFFICULT TO FIND.
THEY ARE, INDEED. UNLIKE THE OCTOPI WE COMMONLY SEE IN AQUARIUMS, THIS PARTICULAR ANIMAL IS SELDOM ENCOUNTERED AND OFTEN FOUND IN THE DEEPEST REACHES OF THE SEA.
AS YOU CAN SEE FROM THESE IMAGES, THE DUMBO OCTOPUS LOOKS MORE LIKE A CHILD'S TOY.
THE DUMBO OCTOPUS, LIKE OTHER OCTOPI, HAS EIGHT ARMS AND LARGE EYES.
WHAT SEPARATES IT FROM OTHER SPECIES IS THE UNUSUAL FINS ON THE SIDE OF ITS HEAD, WHICH IT FLAPS LIKE THE CARTOON CHARACTER DUMBO, THE FLYING ELEPHANT.
THAT'S HOW IT GOT ITS NAME.
VERY COOL!

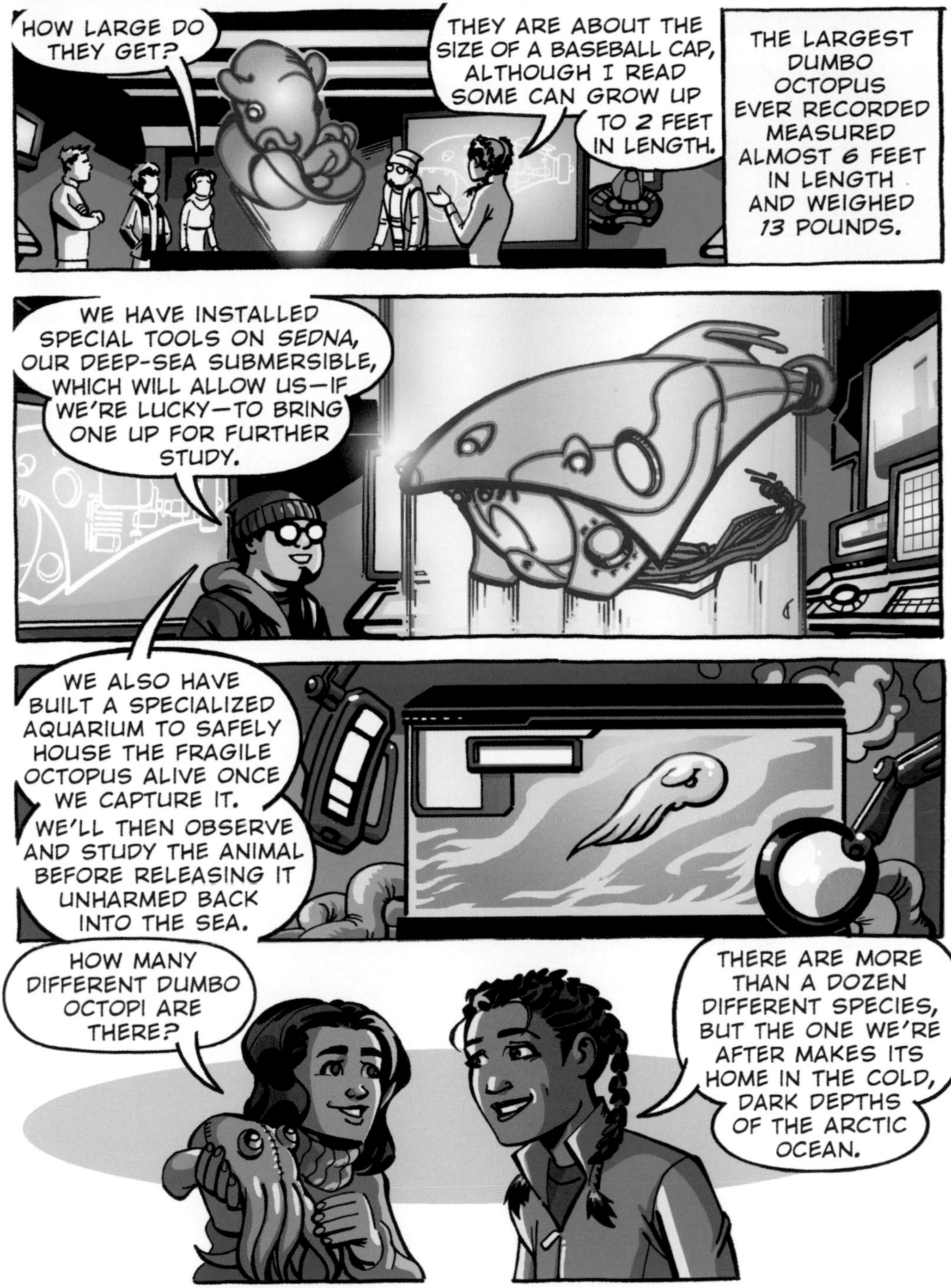
HOW LARGE DO THEY GET?
THEY ARE ABOUT THE SIZE OF A BASEBALL CAP, ALTHOUGH I READ SOME CAN GROW UP TO 2 FEET IN LENGTH.
THE LARGEST DUMBO OCTOPUS EVER RECORDED MEASURED ALMOST 6 FEET IN LENGTH AND WEIGHED 13 POUNDS.
WE HAVE INSTALLED SPECIAL TOOLS ON SEDNA, OUR DEEP-SEA SUBMERSIBLE, WHICH WILL ALLOW US—IF WE'RE LUCKY—TO BRING ONE UP FOR FURTHER STUDY.
WE ALSO HAVE BUILT A SPECIALIZED AQUARIUM TO SAFELY HOUSE THE FRAGILE OCTOPUS ALIVE ONCE WE CAPTURE IT.
WE'LL THEN OBSERVE AND STUDY THE ANIMAL BEFORE RELEASING IT UNHARMED BACK INTO THE SEA.
HOW MANY DIFFERENT DUMBO OCTOPI ARE THERE?
THERE ARE MORE THAN A DOZEN DIFFERENT SPECIES, BUT THE ONE WE'RE AFTER MAKES ITS HOME IN THE COLD, DARK DEPTHS OF THE ARCTIC OCEAN.

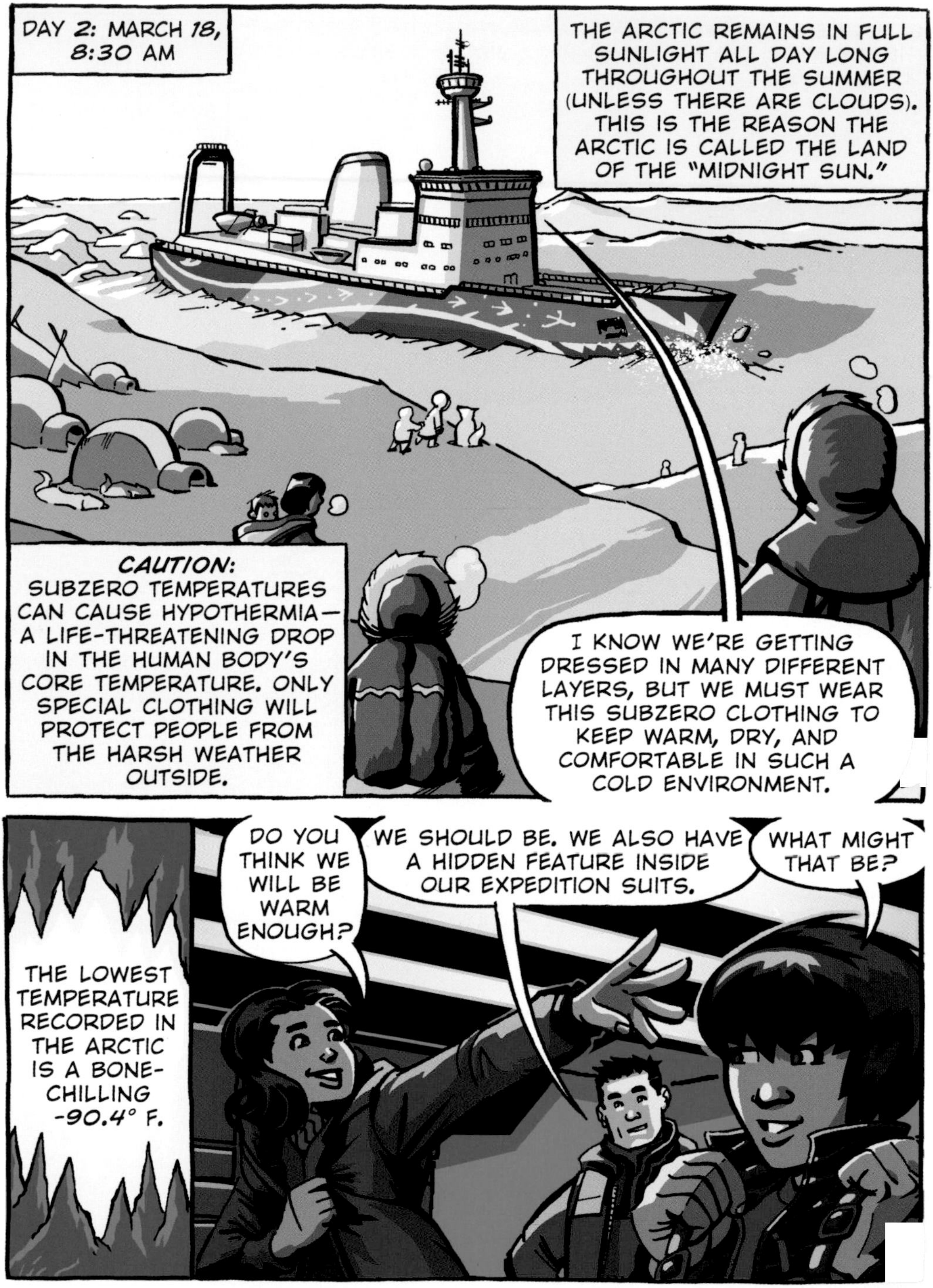
DAY 2: MARCH 18, 8:30 AM
THE ARCTIC REMAINS IN FULL SUNLIGHT ALL DAY LONG THROUGHOUT THE SUMMER (UNLESS THERE ARE CLOUDS). THIS IS THE REASON THE ARCTIC IS CALLED THE LAND OF THE "MIDNIGHT SUN."
CAUTION: SUBZERO TEMPERATURES CAN CAUSE HYPOTHERMIA—A LIFE-THREATENING DROP IN THE HUMAN BODY'S CORE TEMPERATURE. ONLY SPECIAL CLOTHING WILL PROTECT PEOPLE FROM THE HARSH WEATHER OUTSIDE.
I KNOW WE'RE GETTING DRESSED IN MANY DIFFERENT LAYERS, BUT WE MUST WEAR THIS SUBZERO CLOTHING TO KEEP WARM, DRY, AND COMFORTABLE IN SUCH A COLD ENVIRONMENT.
THE LOWEST TEMPERATURE RECORDED IN THE ARCTIC IS A BONE-CHILLING -90.4° F.
DO YOU THINK WE WILL BE WARM ENOUGH?
WE SHOULD BE. WE ALSO HAVE A HIDDEN FEATURE INSIDE OUR EXPEDITION SUITS.
WHAT MIGHT THAT BE?

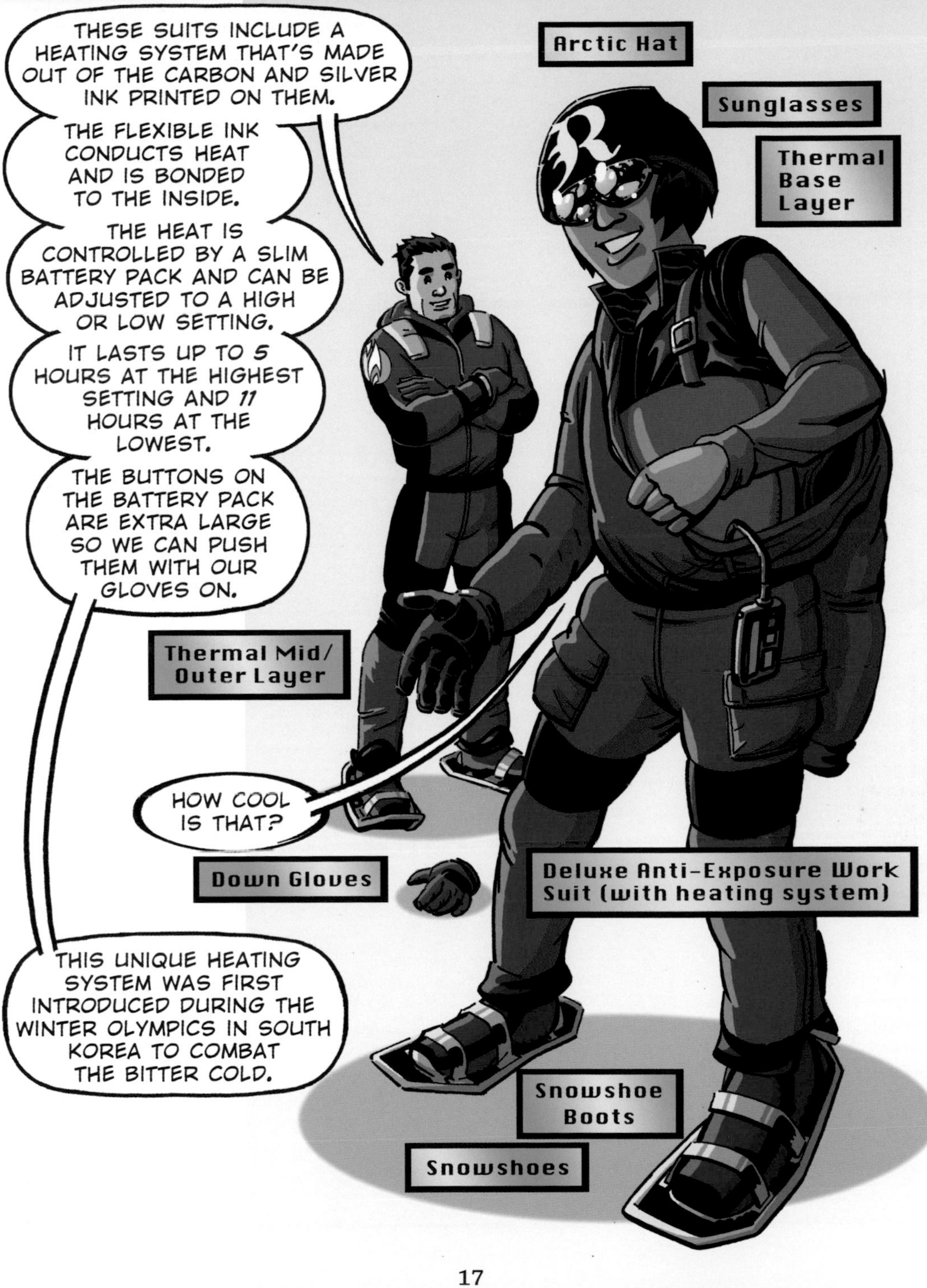
THESE SUITS INCLUDE A HEATING SYSTEM THAT'S MADE OUT OF THE CARBON AND SILVER INK PRINTED ON THEM.
THE FLEXIBLE INK CONDUCTS HEAT AND IS BONDED TO THE INSIDE.
THE HEAT IS CONTROLLED BY A SLIM BATTERY PACK AND CAN BE ADJUSTED TO A HIGH OR LOW SETTING.
IT LASTS UP TO 5 HOURS AT THE HIGHEST SETTING AND 11 HOURS AT THE LOWEST.
THE BUTTONS ON THE BATTERY PACK ARE EXTRA LARGE SO WE CAN PUSH THEM WITH OUR GLOVES ON.
Arctic Hat
Sunglasses
Thermal Base Layer
Thermal Mid/ Outer Layer
HOW COOL IS THAT?
Down Gloves
Deluxe Anti-Exposure Work Suit (with heating system)
THIS UNIQUE HEATING SYSTEM WAS FIRST INTRODUCED DURING THE WINTER OLYMPICS IN SOUTH KOREA TO COMBAT THE BITTER COLD.
Snowshoe Boots
Snowshoes

I CAN'T BELIEVE WE'RE ABOUT TO WALK ON TOP OF THE WORLD!

WHOA!

DO YOU KNOW WHAT'S REALLY COOL? IF YOU STAND AT THE NORTH POLE, WHICHEVER DIRECTION YOU LOOK IS SOUTH.

THAT'S RIGHT! AND REMEMBER, THE ARCTIC OCEAN MAY BE THE SMALLEST AND SHALLOWEST OF THE WORLD'S FIVE MAJOR OCEANS, BUT DON'T LET ITS SIZE FOOL YOU.

THIS OCEAN IS ALMOST THE SIZE OF NORTH AMERICA.

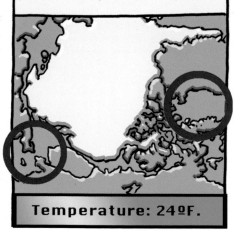

THE ARCTIC OCEAN COVERS 5.4 MILLION SQUARE MILES AND IS LARGER THAN EUROPE. IT'S ALSO CONNECTED TO THE PACIFIC OCEAN BY THE BERING STRAIT AND TO THE ATLANTIC OCEAN BY THE GREENLAND SEA.

Temperature: 24ºF.

WELCOME TO THE LAND BELOW THE ARCTIC CIRCLE, A PLACE OF FAIRY TALES AND FOLKLORE...AND A LARGELY UNEXPLORED PART OF THE WORLD!

I'M LOOKING FORWARD TO WHAT'S IN STORE!

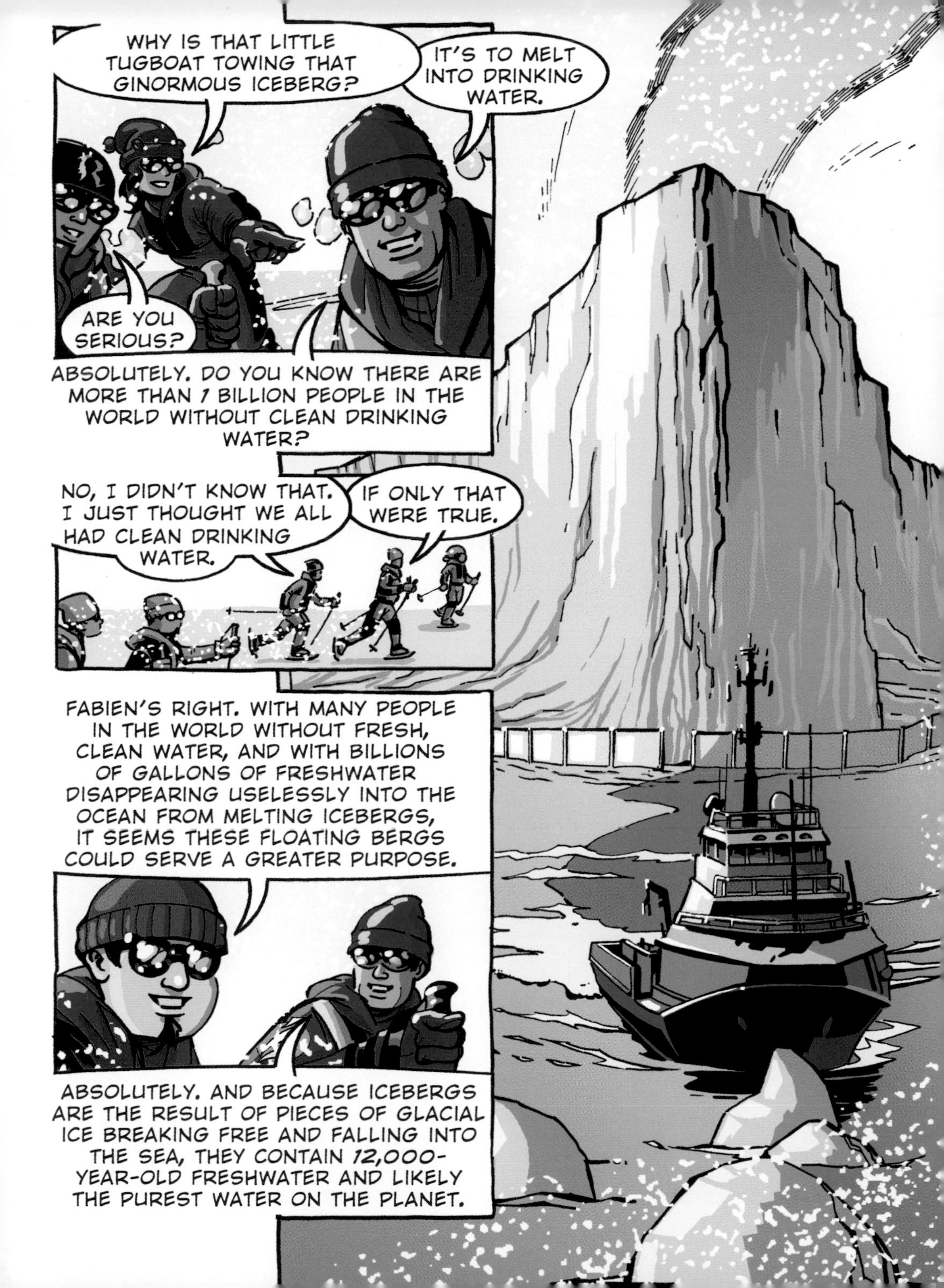
WHY IS THAT LITTLE TUGBOAT TOWING THAT GINORMOUS ICEBERG?
IT'S TO MELT INTO DRINKING WATER.
ARE YOU SERIOUS?
ABSOLUTELY. DO YOU KNOW THERE ARE MORE THAN 1 BILLION PEOPLE IN THE WORLD WITHOUT CLEAN DRINKING WATER?
NO, I DIDN'T KNOW THAT. I JUST THOUGHT WE ALL HAD CLEAN DRINKING WATER.
IF ONLY THAT WERE TRUE.
FABIEN'S RIGHT. WITH MANY PEOPLE IN THE WORLD WITHOUT FRESH, CLEAN WATER, AND WITH BILLIONS OF GALLONS OF FRESHWATER DISAPPEARING USELESSLY INTO THE OCEAN FROM MELTING ICEBERGS, IT SEEMS THESE FLOATING BERGS COULD SERVE A GREATER PURPOSE.
ABSOLUTELY. AND BECAUSE ICEBERGS ARE THE RESULT OF PIECES OF GLACIAL ICE BREAKING FREE AND FALLING INTO THE SEA, THEY CONTAIN 12,000-YEAR-OLD FRESHWATER AND LIKELY THE PUREST WATER ON THE PLANET.

21

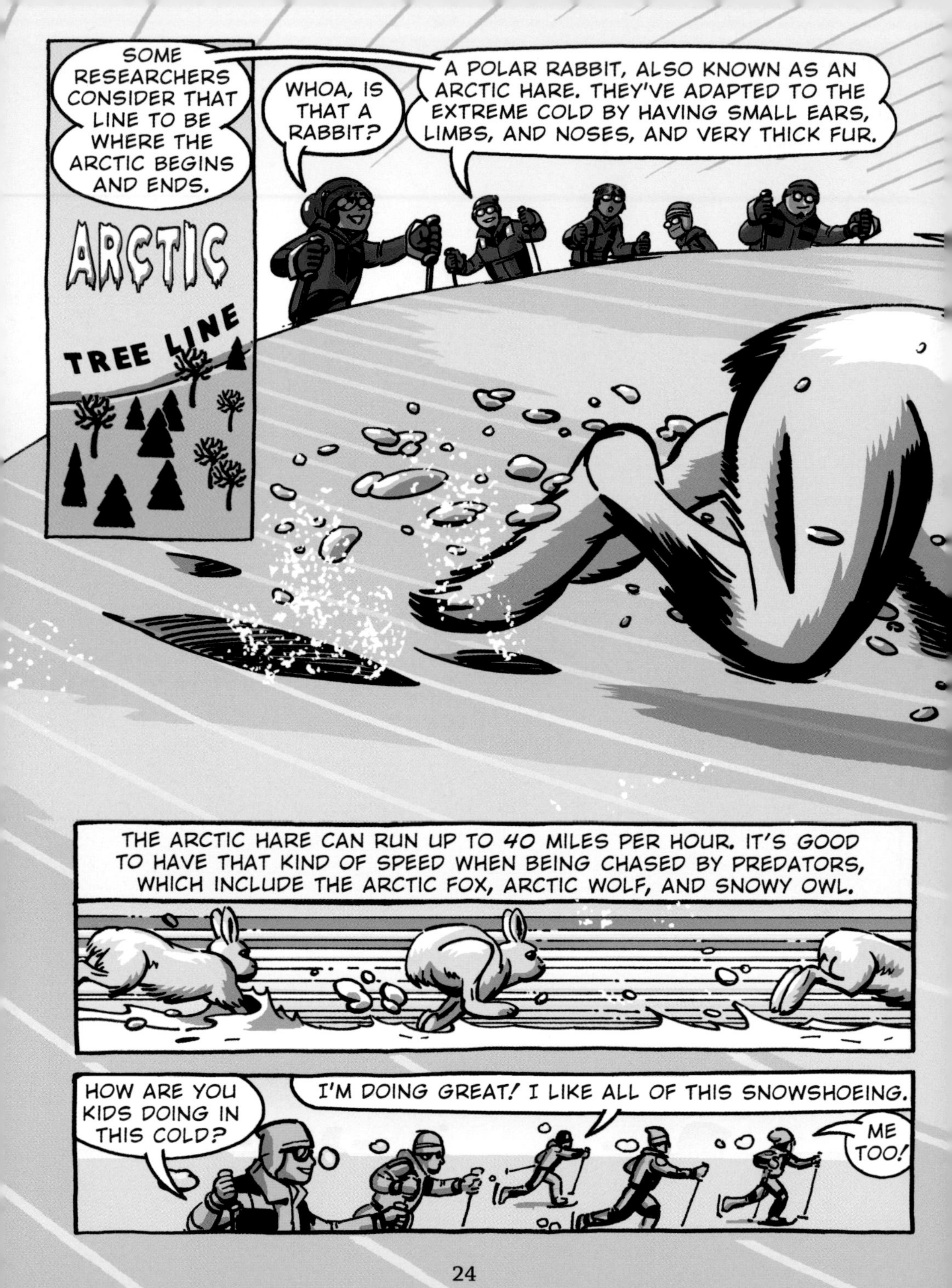
SOME RESEARCHERS CONSIDER THAT LINE TO BE WHERE THE ARCTIC BEGINS AND ENDS.
WHOA, IS THAT A RABBIT?
A POLAR RABBIT, ALSO KNOWN AS AN ARCTIC HARE. THEY'VE ADAPTED TO THE EXTREME COLD BY HAVING SMALL EARS, LIMBS, AND NOSES, AND VERY THICK FUR.
ARCTIC
TREE LINE
THE ARCTIC HARE CAN RUN UP TO 40 MILES PER HOUR. IT'S GOOD TO HAVE THAT KIND OF SPEED WHEN BEING CHASED BY PREDATORS, WHICH INCLUDE THE ARCTIC FOX, ARCTIC WOLF, AND SNOWY OWL.
HOW ARE YOU KIDS DOING IN THIS COLD?
I'M DOING GREAT! I LIKE ALL OF THIS SNOWSHOEING.
ME TOO!

THEY ALSO LIKE TO DIG HOLES UNDER THE SNOW TO KEEP WARM WHILE THEY SLEEP.
SPEAKING OF SNOWSHOEING, DO YOU KNOW IF WE AVOIDED DRIVING JUST 10 MILES EVERY WEEK, AND WALKED INSTEAD, WE WOULD ELIMINATE 500 POUNDS OF CARBON DIOXIDE FROM ENTERING THE ATMOSPHERE?
REALLY? THAT MUCH?
YOU BET! DRIVING CARS, CUTTING DOWN TREES, AND OPERATING FACTORIES ARE JUST A FEW EXAMPLES OF ACTIVITIES THAT FORCE LARGE AMOUNTS OF CARBON DIOXIDE INTO THE AIR.

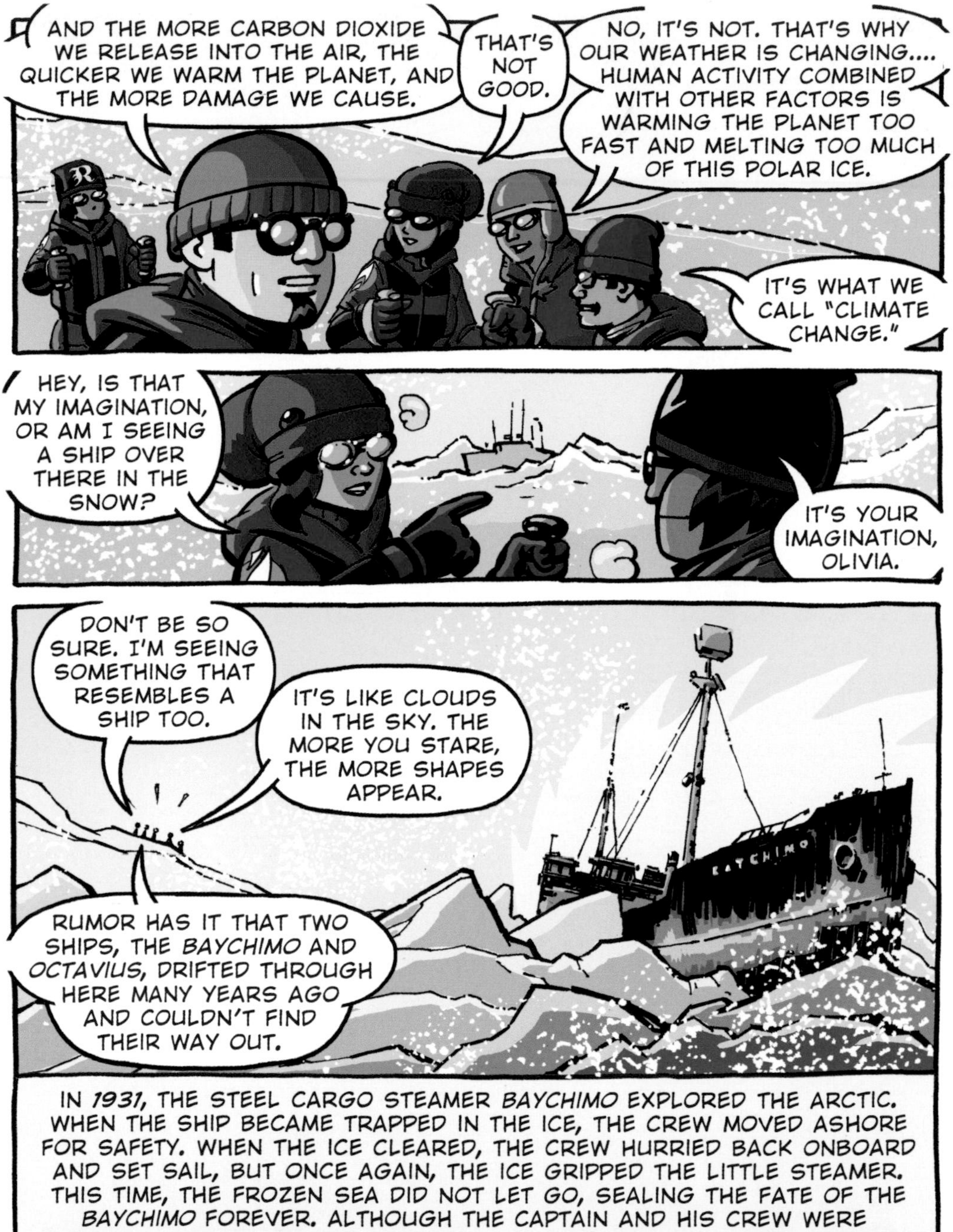
AND THE MORE CARBON DIOXIDE WE RELEASE INTO THE AIR, THE QUICKER WE WARM THE PLANET, AND THE MORE DAMAGE WE CAUSE.
THAT'S NOT GOOD.
NO, IT'S NOT. THAT'S WHY OUR WEATHER IS CHANGING.... HUMAN ACTIVITY COMBINED WITH OTHER FACTORS IS WARMING THE PLANET TOO FAST AND MELTING TOO MUCH OF THIS POLAR ICE.
IT'S WHAT WE CALL "CLIMATE CHANGE."
HEY, IS THAT MY IMAGINATION, OR AM I SEEING A SHIP OVER THERE IN THE SNOW?
IT'S YOUR IMAGINATION, OLIVIA.
DON'T BE SO SURE. I'M SEEING SOMETHING THAT RESEMBLES A SHIP TOO.
IT'S LIKE CLOUDS IN THE SKY. THE MORE YOU STARE, THE MORE SHAPES APPEAR.
RUMOR HAS IT THAT TWO SHIPS, THE *BAYCHIMO* AND *OCTAVIUS*, DRIFTED THROUGH HERE MANY YEARS AGO AND COULDN'T FIND THEIR WAY OUT.
BAYCHIMO
IN *1931*, THE STEEL CARGO STEAMER *BAYCHIMO* EXPLORED THE ARCTIC. WHEN THE SHIP BECAME TRAPPED IN THE ICE, THE CREW MOVED ASHORE FOR SAFETY. WHEN THE ICE CLEARED, THE CREW HURRIED BACK ONBOARD AND SET SAIL, BUT ONCE AGAIN, THE ICE GRIPPED THE LITTLE STEAMER. THIS TIME, THE FROZEN SEA DID NOT LET *GO*, SEALING THE FATE OF THE *BAYCHIMO* FOREVER. ALTHOUGH THE CAPTAIN AND HIS CREW WERE EVENTUALLY RESCUED, THE STEAMER WAS LEFT BEHIND, WHERE—LEGEND HAS IT—IT CONTINUES TO DRIFT AMONG THE ICE BY ITSELF.

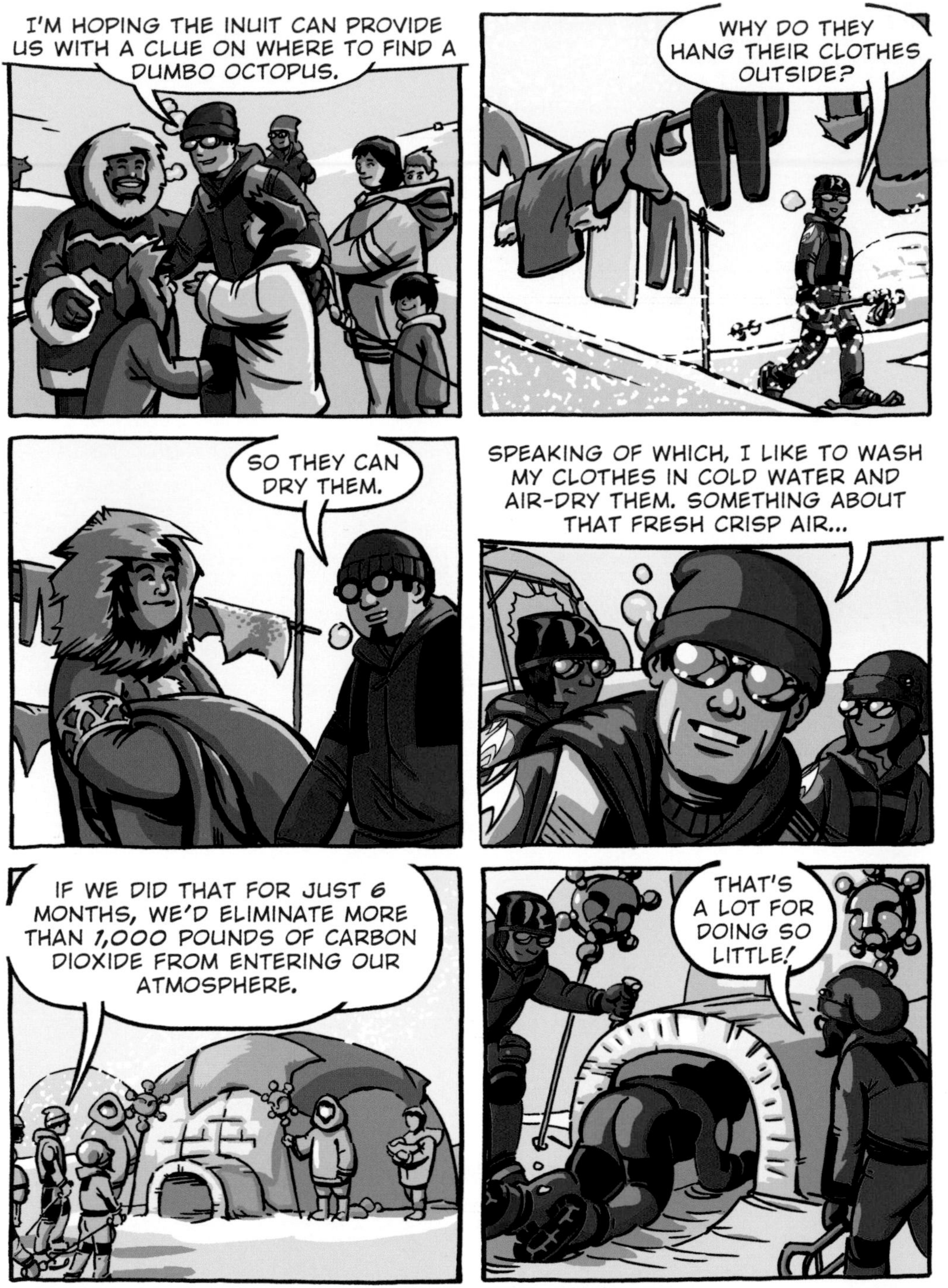
I'M HOPING THE INUIT CAN PROVIDE US WITH A CLUE ON WHERE TO FIND A DUMBO OCTOPUS.
WHY DO THEY HANG THEIR CLOTHES OUTSIDE?
SO THEY CAN DRY THEM.
SPEAKING OF WHICH, I LIKE TO WASH MY CLOTHES IN COLD WATER AND AIR-DRY THEM. SOMETHING ABOUT THAT FRESH CRISP AIR...
IF WE DID THAT FOR JUST 6 MONTHS, WE'D ELIMINATE MORE THAN 1,000 POUNDS OF CARBON DIOXIDE FROM ENTERING OUR ATMOSPHERE.
THAT'S A LOT FOR DOING SO LITTLE!

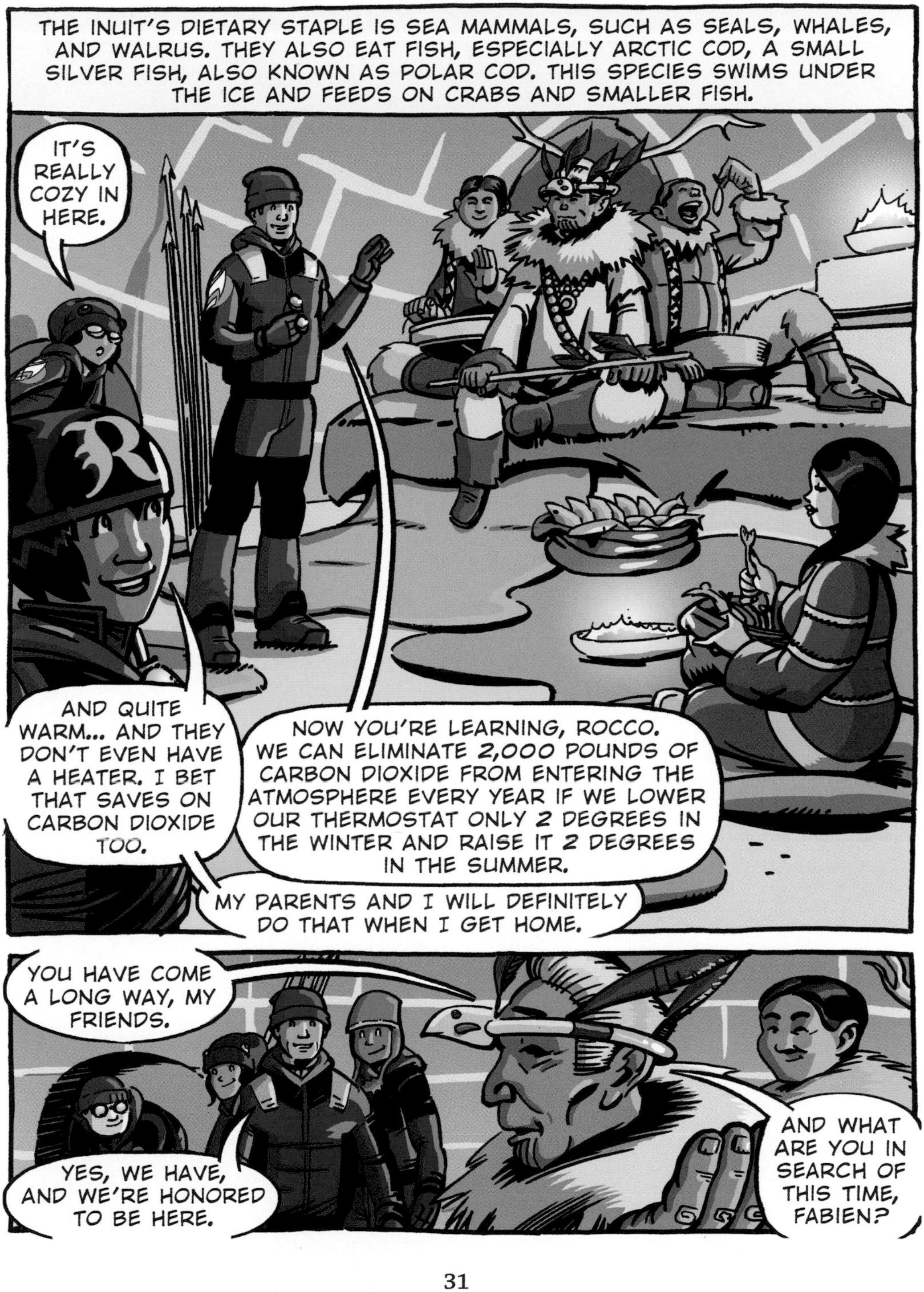
THE INUIT'S DIETARY STAPLE IS SEA MAMMALS, SUCH AS SEALS, WHALES, AND WALRUS. THEY ALSO EAT FISH, ESPECIALLY ARCTIC COD, A SMALL SILVER FISH, ALSO KNOWN AS POLAR COD. THIS SPECIES SWIMS UNDER THE ICE AND FEEDS ON CRABS AND SMALLER FISH.
IT'S REALLY COZY IN HERE.
AND QUITE WARM... AND THEY DON'T EVEN HAVE A HEATER. I BET THAT SAVES ON CARBON DIOXIDE TOO.
NOW YOU'RE LEARNING, ROCCO. WE CAN ELIMINATE 2,000 POUNDS OF CARBON DIOXIDE FROM ENTERING THE ATMOSPHERE EVERY YEAR IF WE LOWER OUR THERMOSTAT ONLY 2 DEGREES IN THE WINTER AND RAISE IT 2 DEGREES IN THE SUMMER.
MY PARENTS AND I WILL DEFINITELY DO THAT WHEN I GET HOME.
YOU HAVE COME A LONG WAY, MY FRIENDS.
YES, WE HAVE, AND WE'RE HONORED TO BE HERE.
AND WHAT ARE YOU IN SEARCH OF THIS TIME, FABIEN?

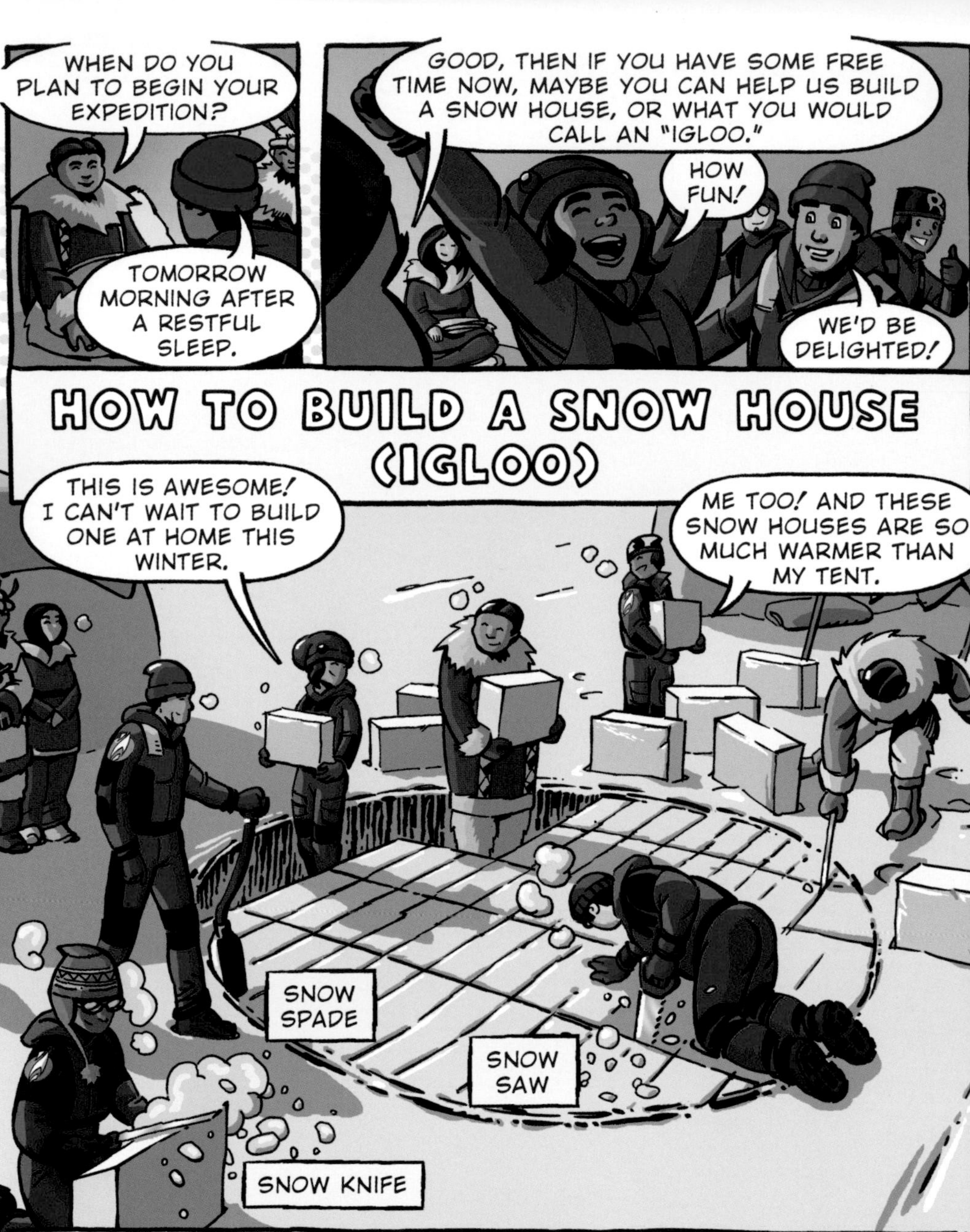
WHEN DO YOU PLAN TO BEGIN YOUR EXPEDITION?
TOMORROW MORNING AFTER A RESTFUL SLEEP.
GOOD, THEN IF YOU HAVE SOME FREE TIME NOW, MAYBE YOU CAN HELP US BUILD A SNOW HOUSE, OR WHAT YOU WOULD CALL AN "IGLOO."
HOW FUN!
WE'D BE DELIGHTED!
HOW TO BUILD A SNOW HOUSE (IGLOO)
THIS IS AWESOME! I CAN'T WAIT TO BUILD ONE AT HOME THIS WINTER.
ME TOO! AND THESE SNOW HOUSES ARE SO MUCH WARMER THAN MY TENT.
SNOW SPADE
SNOW SAW
SNOW KNIFE

STEP 1: LOCATION

CHOOSE AN AREA WITH HARD, COMPACT SNOW. USING THE SNOW SPADE, MAKE A CIRCLE IN THE SNOW ABOUT THE SIZE OF THE HOUSE YOU WANT TO BUILD, BUT DON'T MAKE IT TOO BIG.

STEP 2: THE BLOCKS

USING THE SNOW SAW, CUT LARGE BLOCKS OUT OF THE SNOW FOR THE BASE OF THE DOME. CUT SMALLER BLOCKS FOR THE TOP. SMOOTH THE EDGES OF EACH BLOCK WITH THE SNOW KNIFE.

STEP 3: BUILDING

STACK THE LARGE BLOCKS TIGHTLY, SIDE BY SIDE, AROUND THE OUTER CIRCLE YOU DREW IN THE SNOW. SLANT THE BLOCKS INWARD—OTHERWISE YOU WILL BE BUILDING A TOWER. FOR THE ENTRANCE, PLACE FOUR BLOCKS POINTING OUTWARD, TWO ON EACH SIDE. USE MORE BLOCKS TO MAKE A SMALL ROOF ON THE ENTRANCE. NOW KEEP ADDING THE BLOCKS TO FILL IN THE CIRCLE, LEAVING AN OPENING TO THE ENTRANCE. MAKE SURE TO REMOVE ALL THE SNOW THAT IS PILING UP INSIDE. THE FINAL BLOCKS CAN BE BROUGHT IN THROUGH THE ENTRANCE AND STACKED FROM INSIDE THE SNOW HOUSE.

STEP 4: FINAL TOUCHES

FILL IN ANY CRACKS BETWEEN THE BLOCKS WITH SNOW FOR A PERFECT SEAL. SMOOTH THE INTERIOR WALLS WITH YOUR GLOVED HANDS. ADD A SMALL HOLE IN THE ROOF SO FRESH AIR CAN COME IN AND OUT. CONGRATULATIONS! YOU'VE BUILT YOUR FIRST SNOW HOUSE (IGLOO).

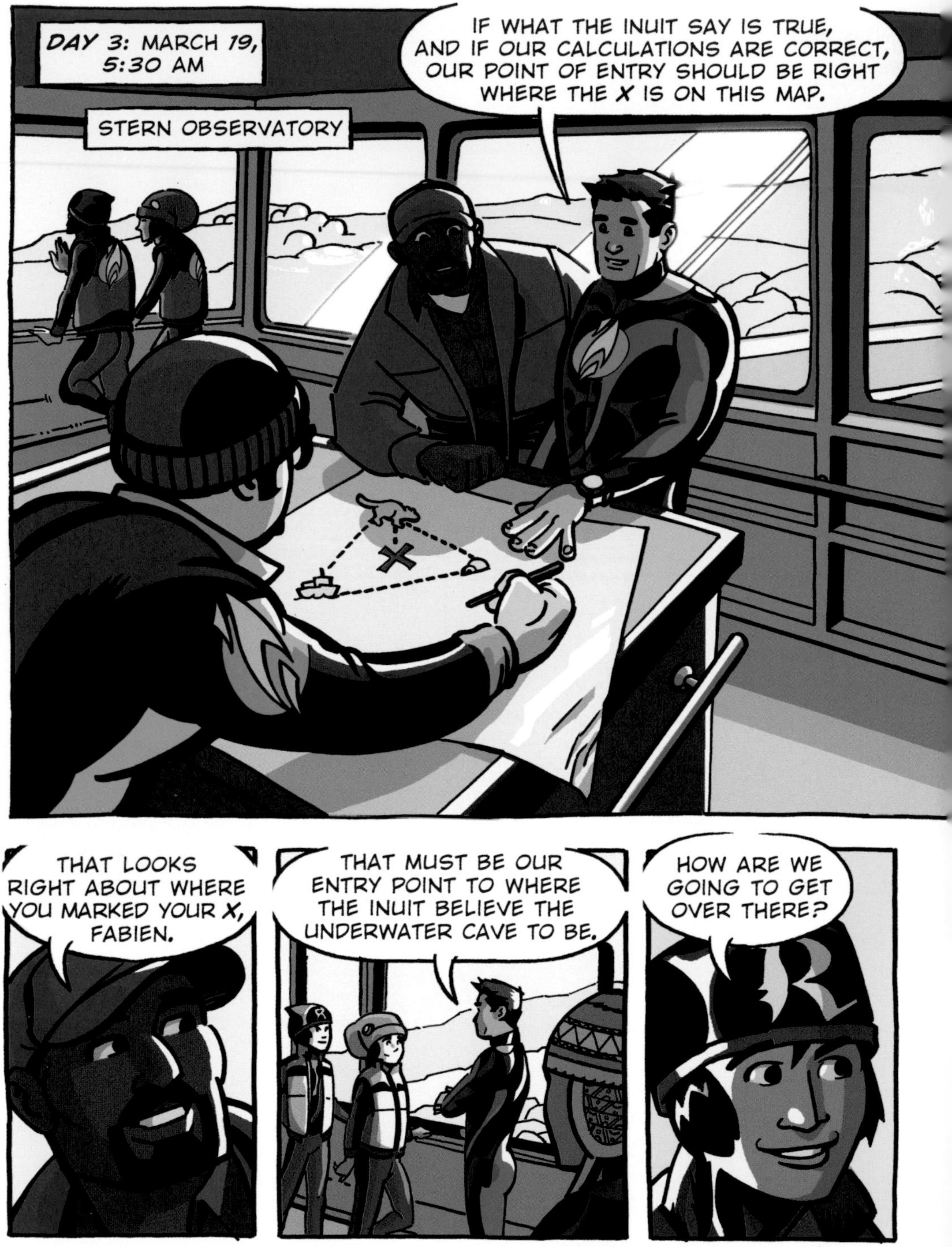
DAY 3: MARCH 19, 5:30 AM
STERN OBSERVATORY
IF WHAT THE INUIT SAY IS TRUE, AND IF OUR CALCULATIONS ARE CORRECT, OUR POINT OF ENTRY SHOULD BE RIGHT WHERE THE X IS ON THIS MAP.
THAT LOOKS RIGHT ABOUT WHERE YOU MARKED YOUR X, FABIEN.
THAT MUST BE OUR ENTRY POINT TO WHERE THE INUIT BELIEVE THE UNDERWATER CAVE TO BE.
HOW ARE WE GOING TO GET OVER THERE?

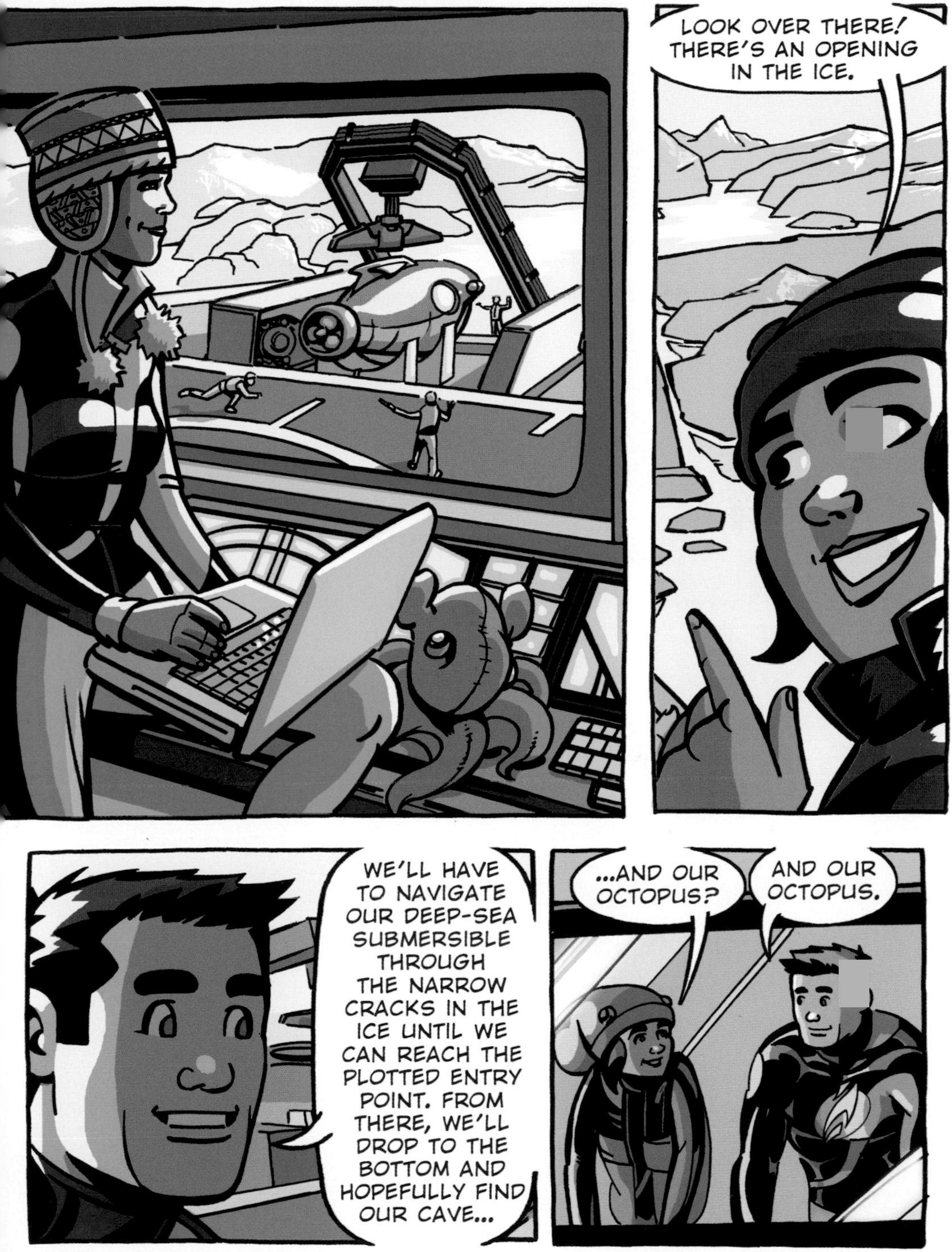
LOOK OVER THERE! THERE'S AN OPENING IN THE ICE.
WE'LL HAVE TO NAVIGATE OUR DEEP-SEA SUBMERSIBLE THROUGH THE NARROW CRACKS IN THE ICE UNTIL WE CAN REACH THE PLOTTED ENTRY POINT. FROM THERE, WE'LL DROP TO THE BOTTOM AND HOPEFULLY FIND OUR CAVE...
...AND OUR OCTOPUS?
AND OUR OCTOPUS.

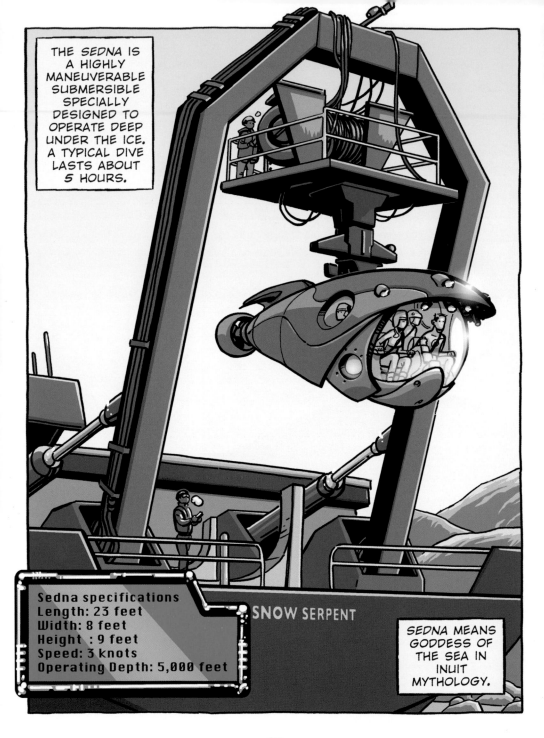

THE SEDNA IS A HIGHLY MANEUVERABLE SUBMERSIBLE SPECIALLY DESIGNED TO OPERATE DEEP UNDER THE ICE. A TYPICAL DIVE LASTS ABOUT 5 HOURS.

SNOW SERPENT

Sedna specifications
Length: 23 feet
Width: 8 feet
Height : 9 feet
Speed: 3 knots
Operating Depth: 5,000 feet

SEDNA MEANS GODDESS OF THE SEA IN INUIT MYTHOLOGY.

AS YOU CAN SEE, IT TAKES A CREW TO LAUNCH US INTO THE CHANNEL. THE FIRST IS THE CRANE OPERATOR, WHO JUST LIFTED THE *SEDNA* FROM THE DECK AND GENTLY PLACED HER IN THE WATER. THE SUBMERSIBLE SUPERVISOR OVERSEES THE PROCESS, ALONG WITH THE SUB OPERATIONS COORDINATOR. ANOTHER CREW MEMBER IS IN CHARGE OF HANDLING THE CRANE LINES TO MAKE SURE NOTHING GETS TANGLED UP.

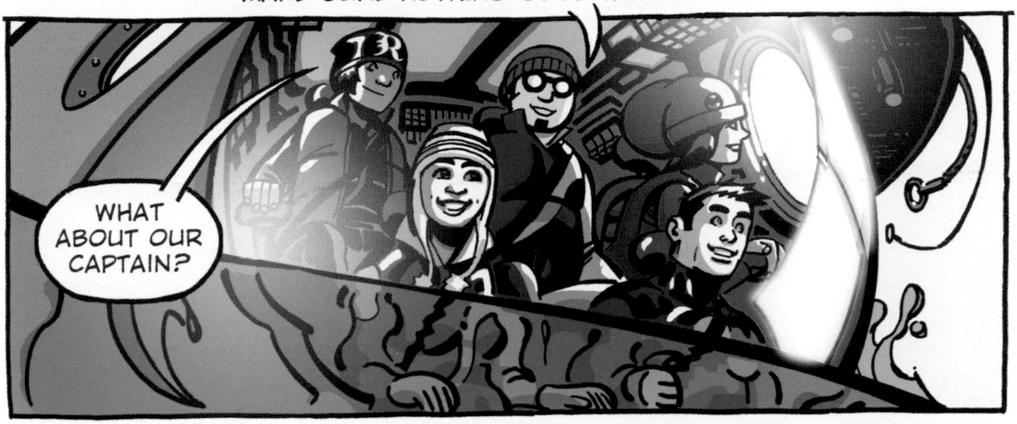
WHAT ABOUT OUR CAPTAIN?

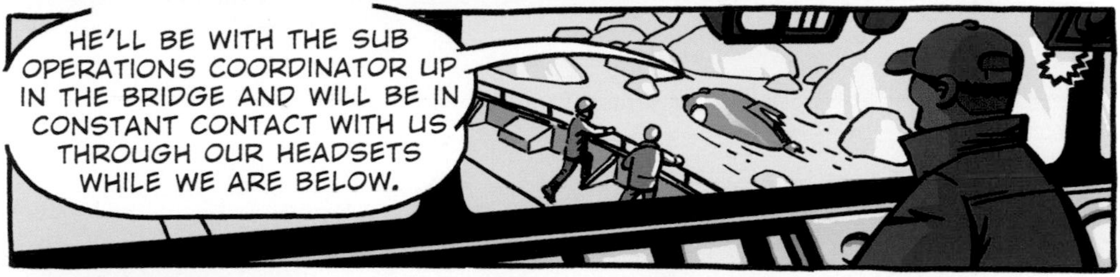
HE'LL BE WITH THE SUB OPERATIONS COORDINATOR UP IN THE BRIDGE AND WILL BE IN CONSTANT CONTACT WITH US THROUGH OUR HEADSETS WHILE WE ARE BELOW.

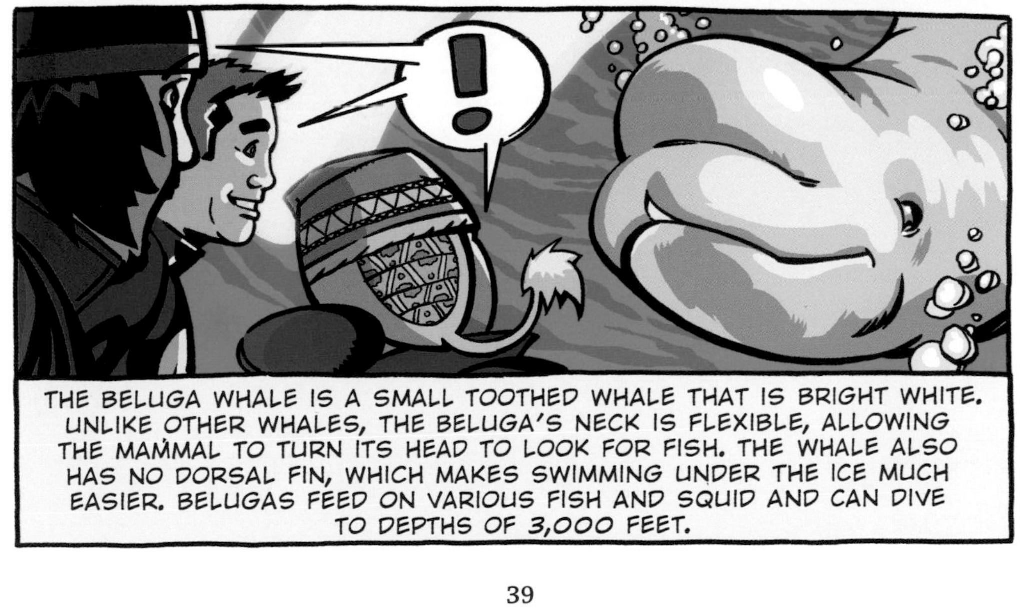
!

THE BELUGA WHALE IS A SMALL TOOTHED WHALE THAT IS BRIGHT WHITE. UNLIKE OTHER WHALES, THE BELUGA'S NECK IS FLEXIBLE, ALLOWING THE MAMMAL TO TURN ITS HEAD TO LOOK FOR FISH. THE WHALE ALSO HAS NO DORSAL FIN, WHICH MAKES SWIMMING UNDER THE ICE MUCH EASIER. BELUGAS FEED ON VARIOUS FISH AND SQUID AND CAN DIVE TO DEPTHS OF 3,000 FEET.

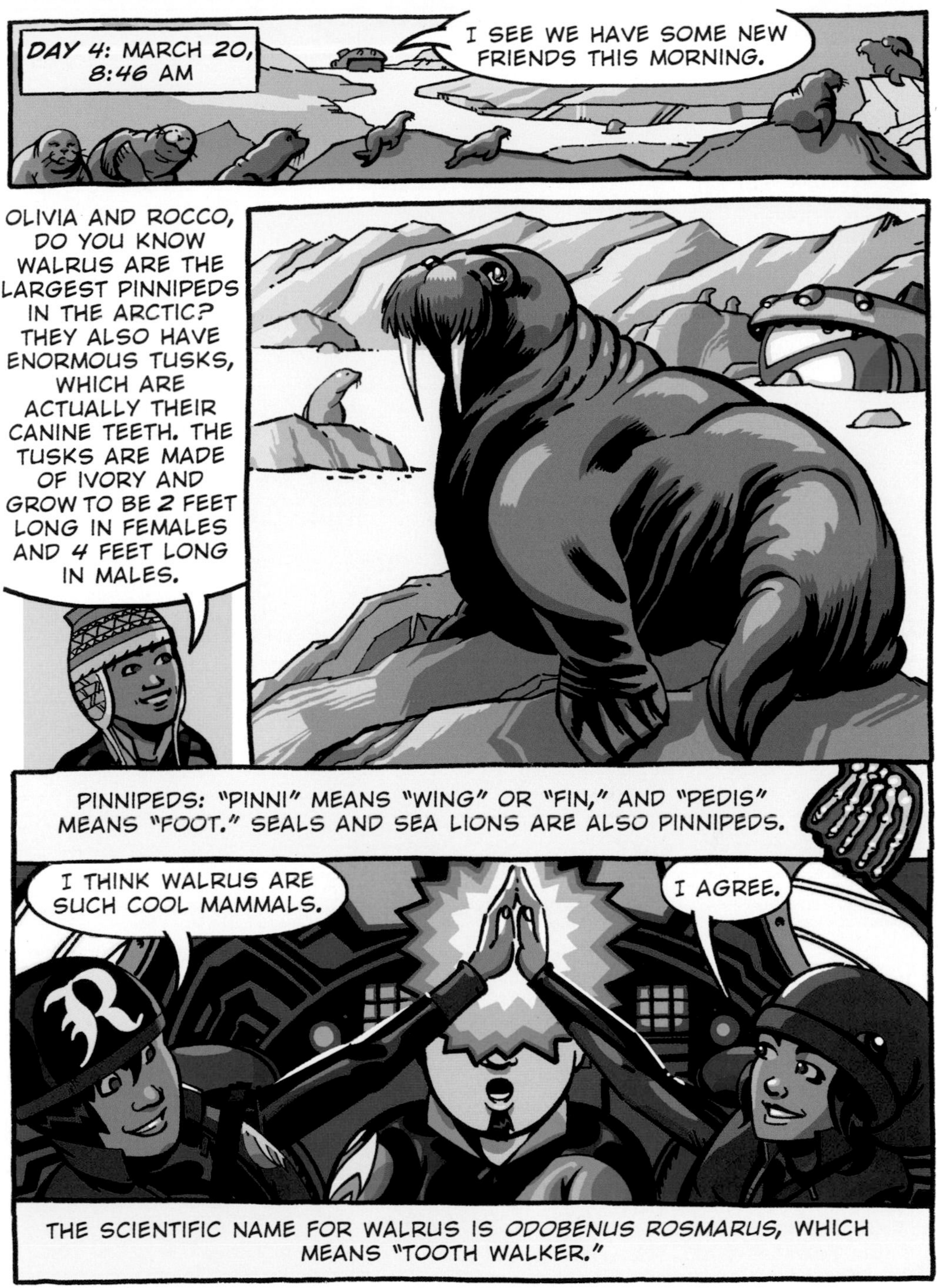
DAY 4: MARCH 20, 8:46 AM
I SEE WE HAVE SOME NEW FRIENDS THIS MORNING.
OLIVIA AND ROCCO, DO YOU KNOW WALRUS ARE THE LARGEST PINNIPEDS IN THE ARCTIC? THEY ALSO HAVE ENORMOUS TUSKS, WHICH ARE ACTUALLY THEIR CANINE TEETH. THE TUSKS ARE MADE OF IVORY AND GROW TO BE 2 FEET LONG IN FEMALES AND 4 FEET LONG IN MALES.
PINNIPEDS: "PINNI" MEANS "WING" OR "FIN," AND "PEDIS" MEANS "FOOT." SEALS AND SEA LIONS ARE ALSO PINNIPEDS.
I THINK WALRUS ARE SUCH COOL MAMMALS.
I AGREE.
THE SCIENTIFIC NAME FOR WALRUS IS *ODOBENUS ROSMARUS*, WHICH MEANS "TOOTH WALKER."

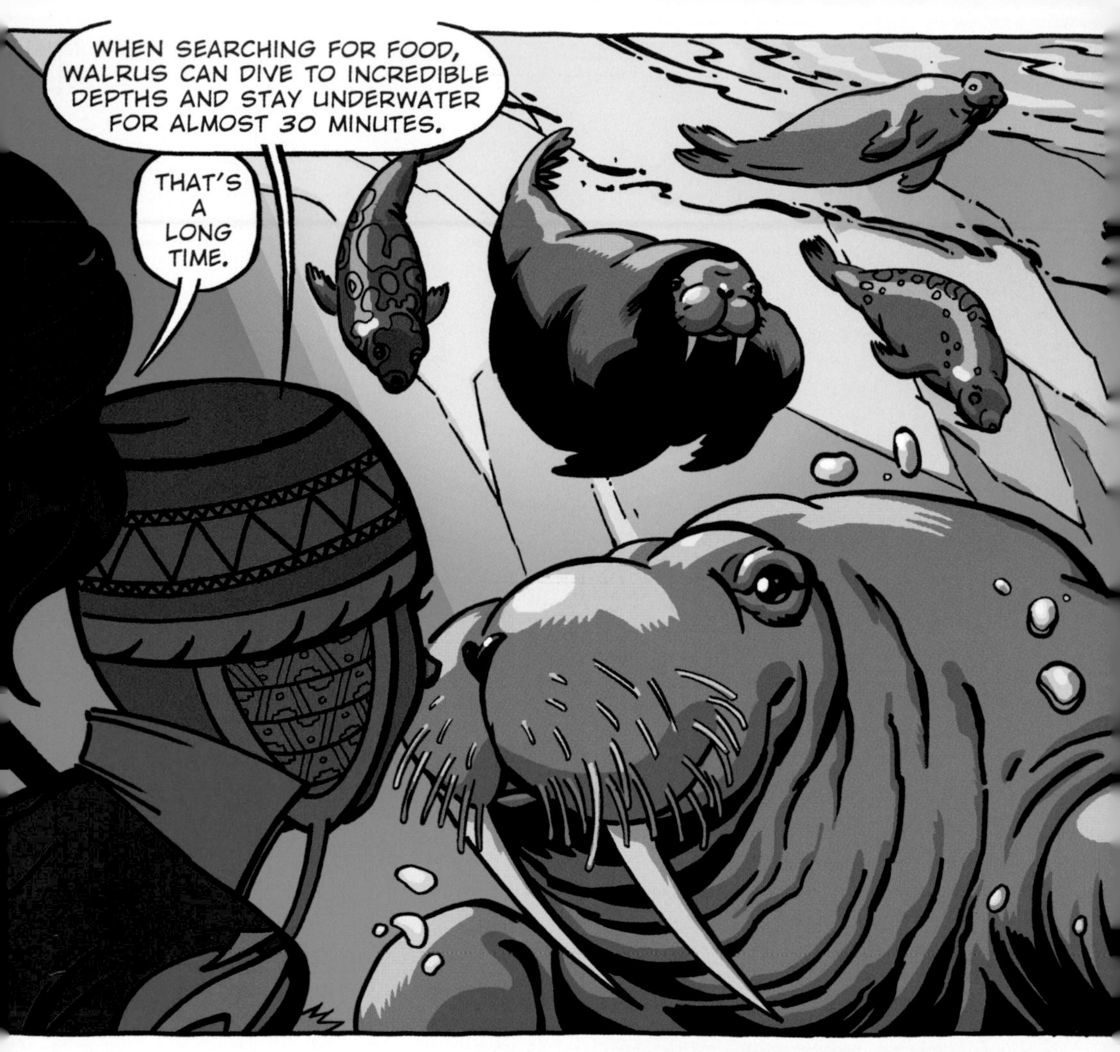
WHEN SEARCHING FOR FOOD, WALRUS CAN DIVE TO INCREDIBLE DEPTHS AND STAY UNDERWATER FOR ALMOST 30 MINUTES.
THAT'S A LONG TIME.

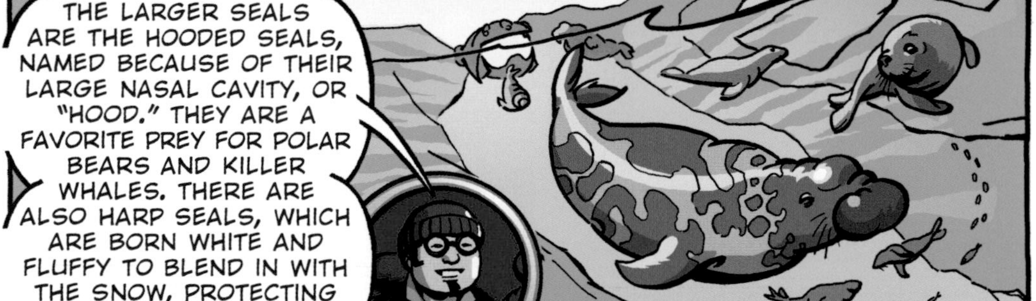
THE LARGER SEALS ARE THE HOODED SEALS, NAMED BECAUSE OF THEIR LARGE NASAL CAVITY, OR "HOOD." THEY ARE A FAVORITE PREY FOR POLAR BEARS AND KILLER WHALES. THERE ARE ALSO HARP SEALS, WHICH ARE BORN WHITE AND FLUFFY TO BLEND IN WITH THE SNOW, PROTECTING THEM FROM PREDATORS.

ICE WORMS WILL LIQUEFY IF EXPOSED TO TEMPERATURES HIGHER THAN 41°F.

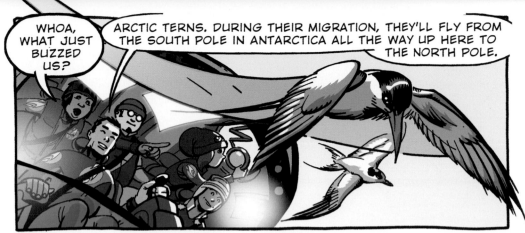

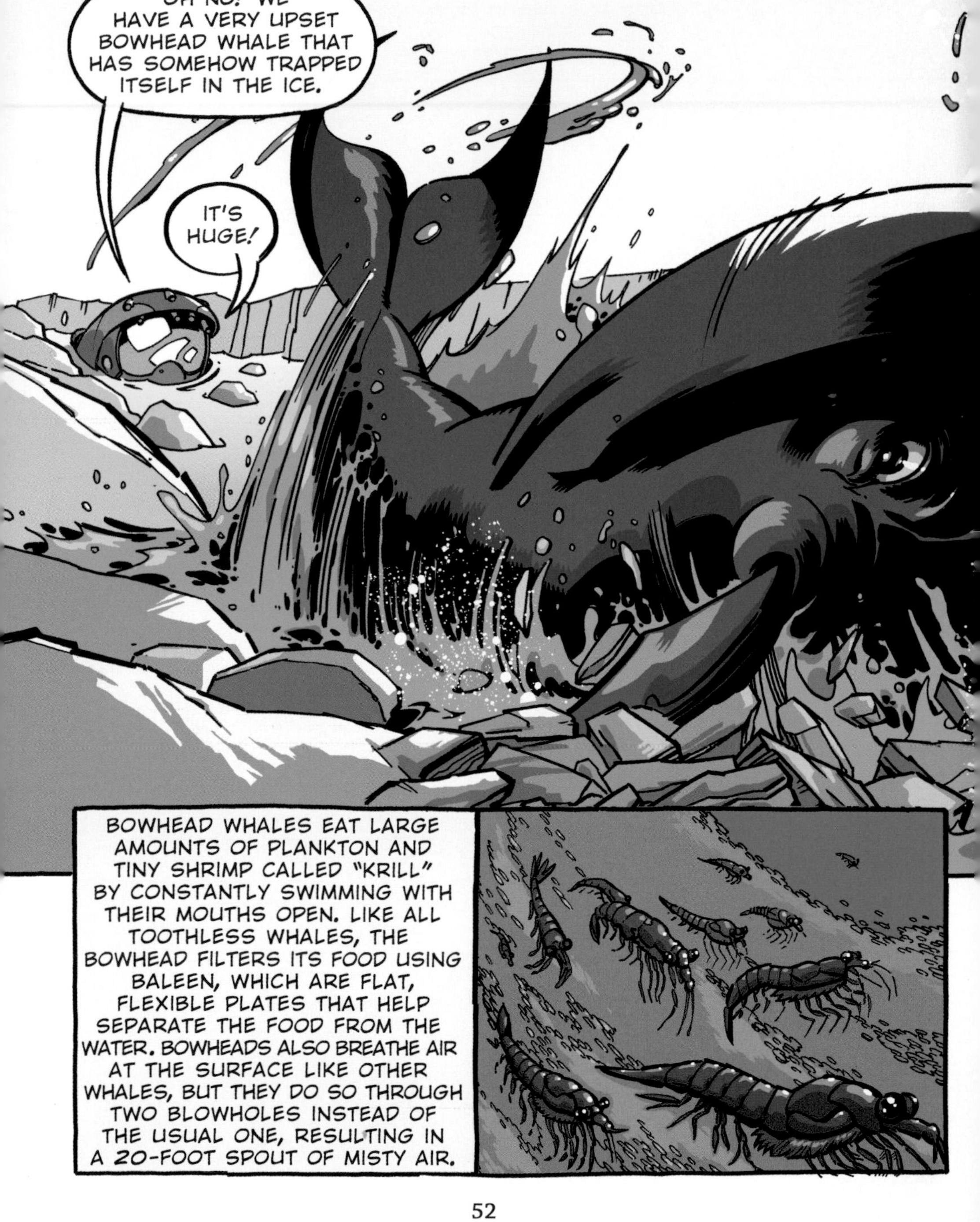
OH NO! WE HAVE A VERY UPSET BOWHEAD WHALE THAT HAS SOMEHOW TRAPPED ITSELF IN THE ICE.
IT'S HUGE!
BOWHEAD WHALES EAT LARGE AMOUNTS OF PLANKTON AND TINY SHRIMP CALLED "KRILL" BY CONSTANTLY SWIMMING WITH THEIR MOUTHS OPEN. LIKE ALL TOOTHLESS WHALES, THE BOWHEAD FILTERS ITS FOOD USING BALEEN, WHICH ARE FLAT, FLEXIBLE PLATES THAT HELP SEPARATE THE FOOD FROM THE WATER. BOWHEADS ALSO BREATHE AIR AT THE SURFACE LIKE OTHER WHALES, BUT THEY DO SO THROUGH TWO BLOWHOLES INSTEAD OF THE USUAL ONE, RESULTING IN A 20-FOOT SPOUT OF MISTY AIR.

WHALES LIKE THE BOWHEAD THRIVE IN THE ARCTIC. HUMPBACKS, BLUES, MINKE, FIN, AND GRAY WHALES ALSO MAKE THE ANNUAL TRIP TO THE NORTH POLE. IN FACT, GRAY WHALES MIGRATE *12,500* MILES FROM THE ARCTIC TO MEXICO AND BACK EVERY YEAR.

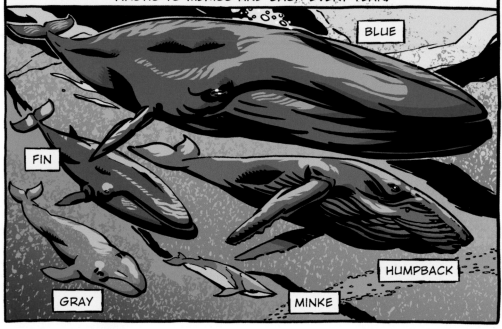

BLUE

FIN

GRAY

MINKE

HUMPBACK

AH, GUYS...? WE HAVE ANOTHER PROBLEM!

THE WHALE'S TALL GEYSER-LIKE SPOUT IS DRAWING ATTENTION, AND THOSE HUNGRY BEARS HAVE PICKED UP ON IT.

THEY'RE SURE IN A HURRY THIS TIME.

THEY MUST BE REALLY HUNGRY.

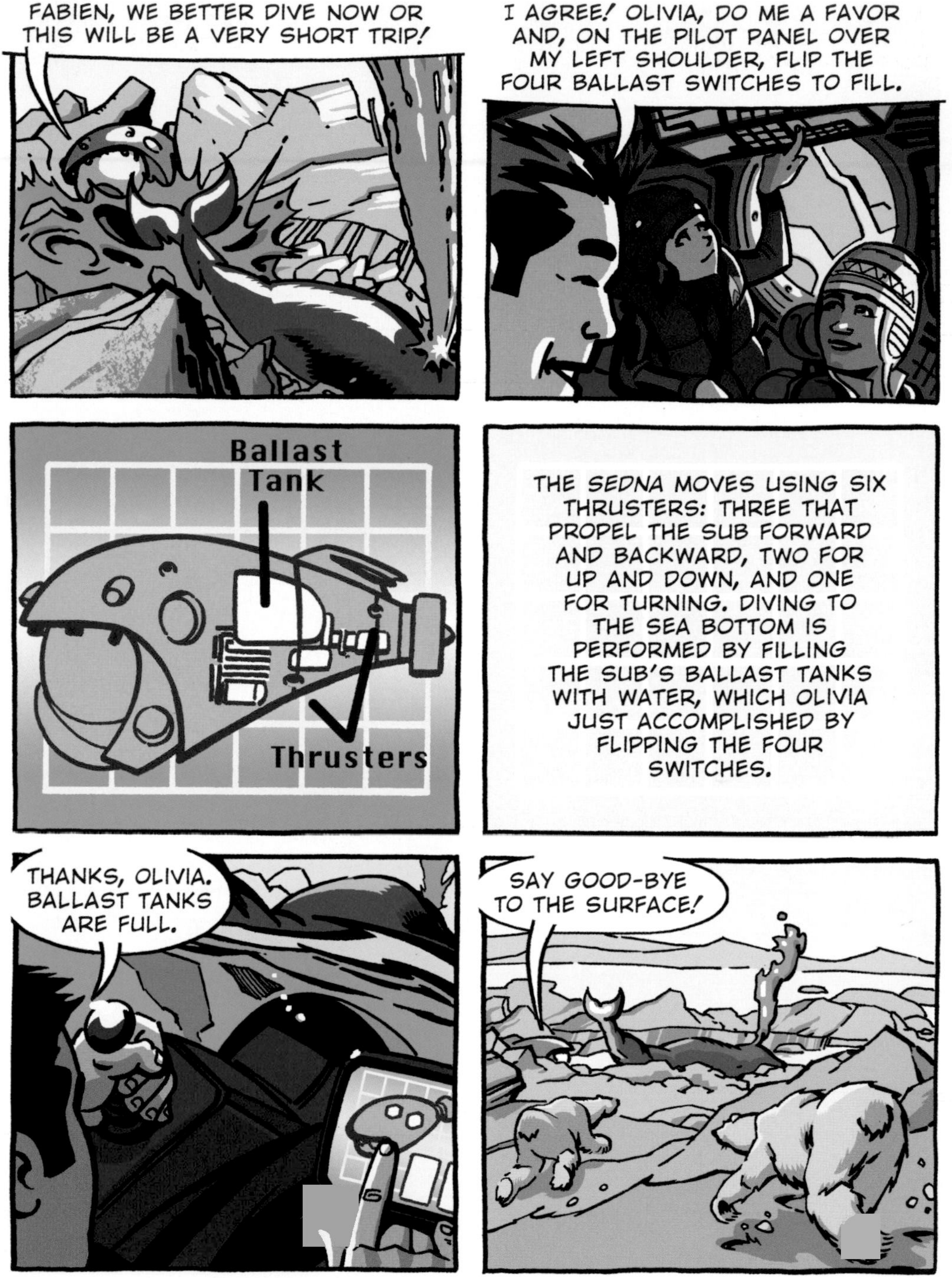
FABIEN, WE BETTER DIVE NOW OR THIS WILL BE A VERY SHORT TRIP!
I AGREE! OLIVIA, DO ME A FAVOR AND, ON THE PILOT PANEL OVER MY LEFT SHOULDER, FLIP THE FOUR BALLAST SWITCHES TO FILL.
Ballast Tank
Thrusters
THE *SEDNA* MOVES USING SIX THRUSTERS: THREE THAT PROPEL THE SUB FORWARD AND BACKWARD, TWO FOR UP AND DOWN, AND ONE FOR TURNING. DIVING TO THE SEA BOTTOM IS PERFORMED BY FILLING THE SUB'S BALLAST TANKS WITH WATER, WHICH OLIVIA JUST ACCOMPLISHED BY FLIPPING THE FOUR SWITCHES.
THANKS, OLIVIA. BALLAST TANKS ARE FULL.
SAY GOOD-BYE TO THE SURFACE!

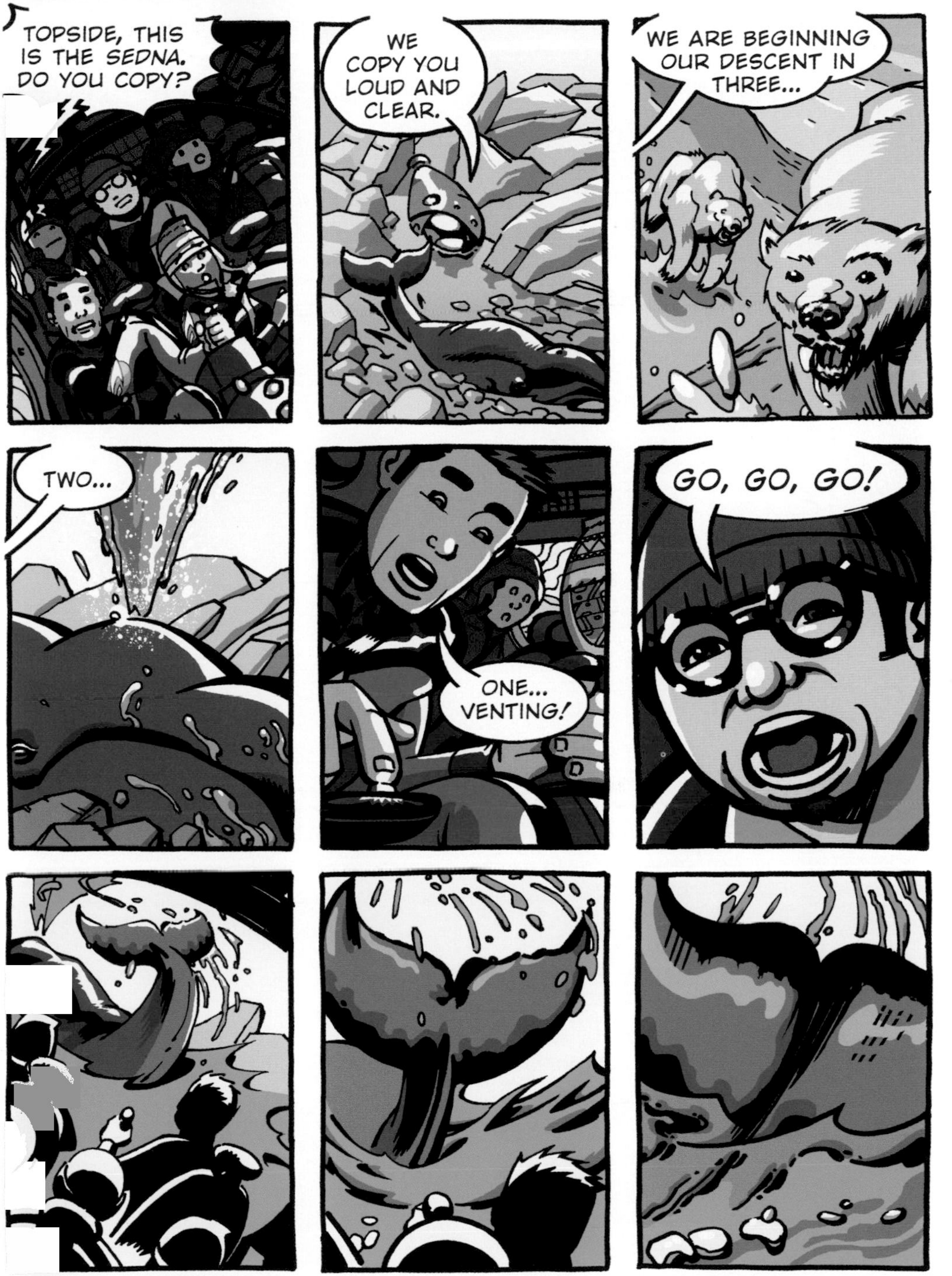
TOPSIDE, THIS IS THE SEDNA. DO YOU COPY?
WE COPY YOU LOUD AND CLEAR.
WE ARE BEGINNING OUR DESCENT IN THREE...
TWO...
ONE... VENTING!
GO, GO, GO!

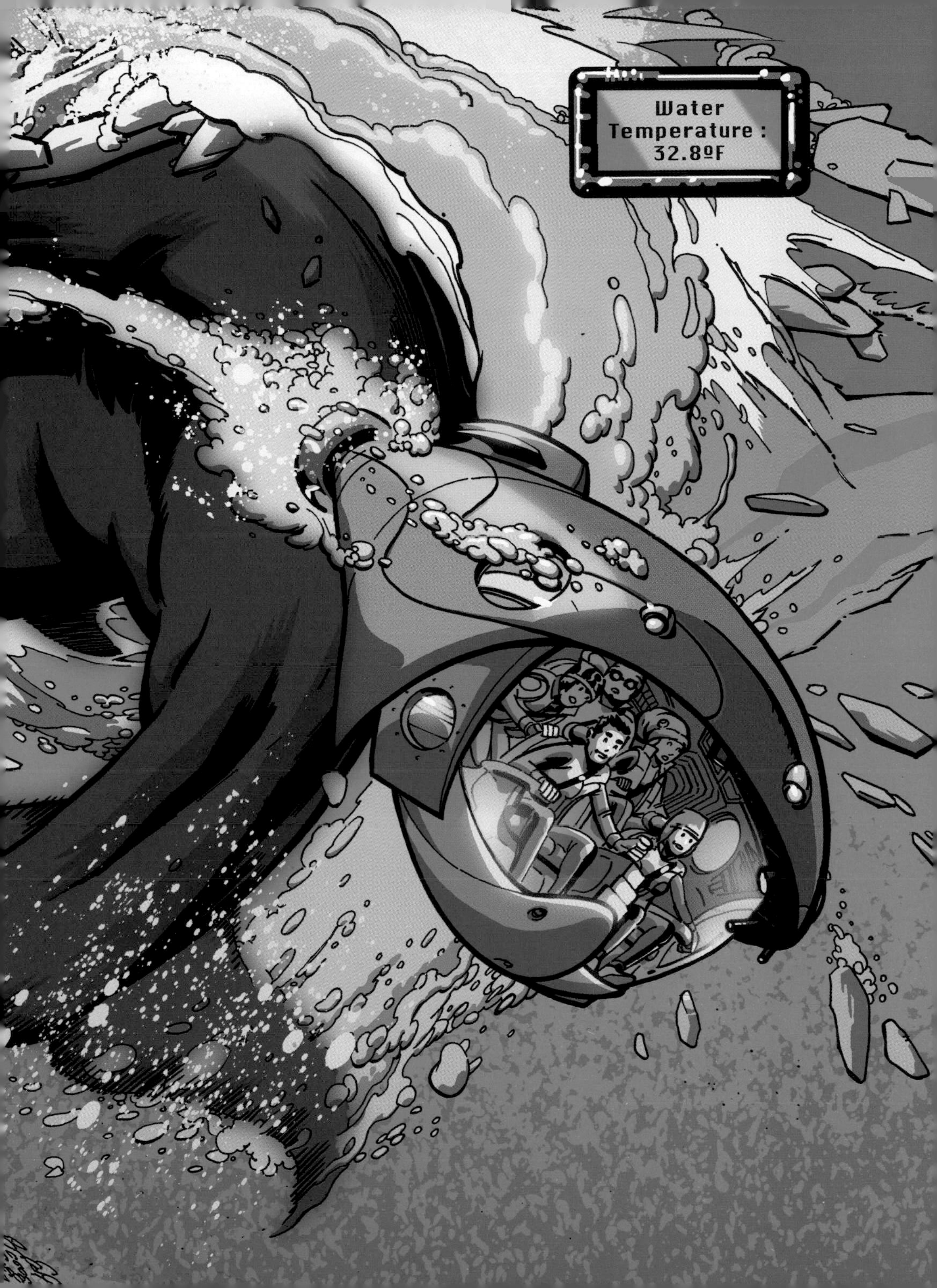
Water
Temperature :
32.8ºF

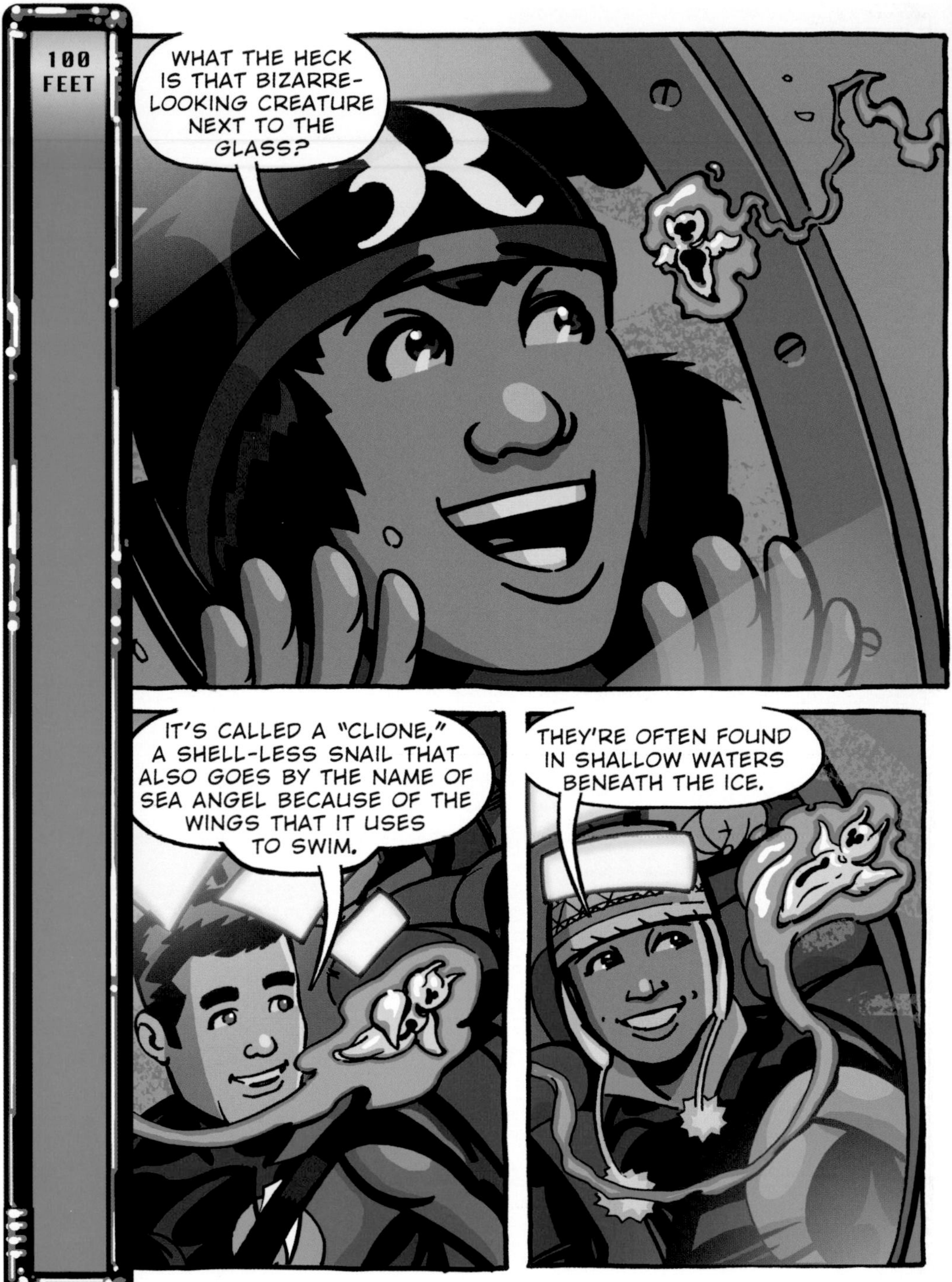
100 FEET
WHAT THE HECK IS THAT BIZARRE-LOOKING CREATURE NEXT TO THE GLASS?
IT'S CALLED A "CLIONE," A SHELL-LESS SNAIL THAT ALSO GOES BY THE NAME OF SEA ANGEL BECAUSE OF THE WINGS THAT IT USES TO SWIM.
THEY'RE OFTEN FOUND IN SHALLOW WATERS BENEATH THE ICE.

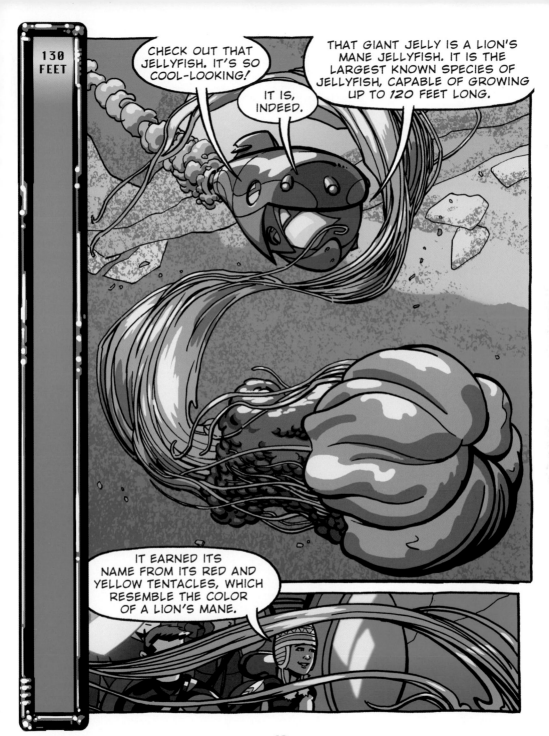

64

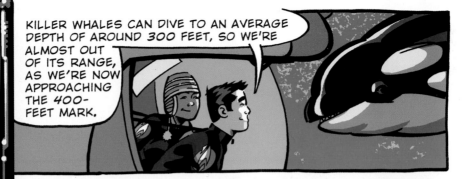

KILLER WHALES CAN DIVE TO AN AVERAGE DEPTH OF AROUND *300* FEET, SO WE'RE ALMOST OUT OF ITS RANGE, AS WE'RE NOW APPROACHING THE *400*-FEET MARK.

KILLER WHALES ARE THE LARGEST MEMBER OF THE DOLPHIN FAMILY AND FEMALES CAN LIVE UP TO *50* YEARS IN THE WILD.

KILLER WHALES ARE ALSO VERY STRONG SWIMMERS AND, LIKE NARWHALS, OFTEN TRAVEL IN GROUPS CALLED PODS. PODS USUALLY CONSIST OF *5* TO *30* WHALES, ALTHOUGH SOME PODS MAY BE AS LARGE AS *100* OR MORE. THIS ONE MUST HAVE LEFT THE POD TO CHECK US OUT.

A MALE KILLER WHALE CAN GROW TO *23* FEET LONG AND WEIGH *7* TO *10* TONS. FEMALES CAN REACH *21* FEET AND WEIGH *4* TO *6* TONS.

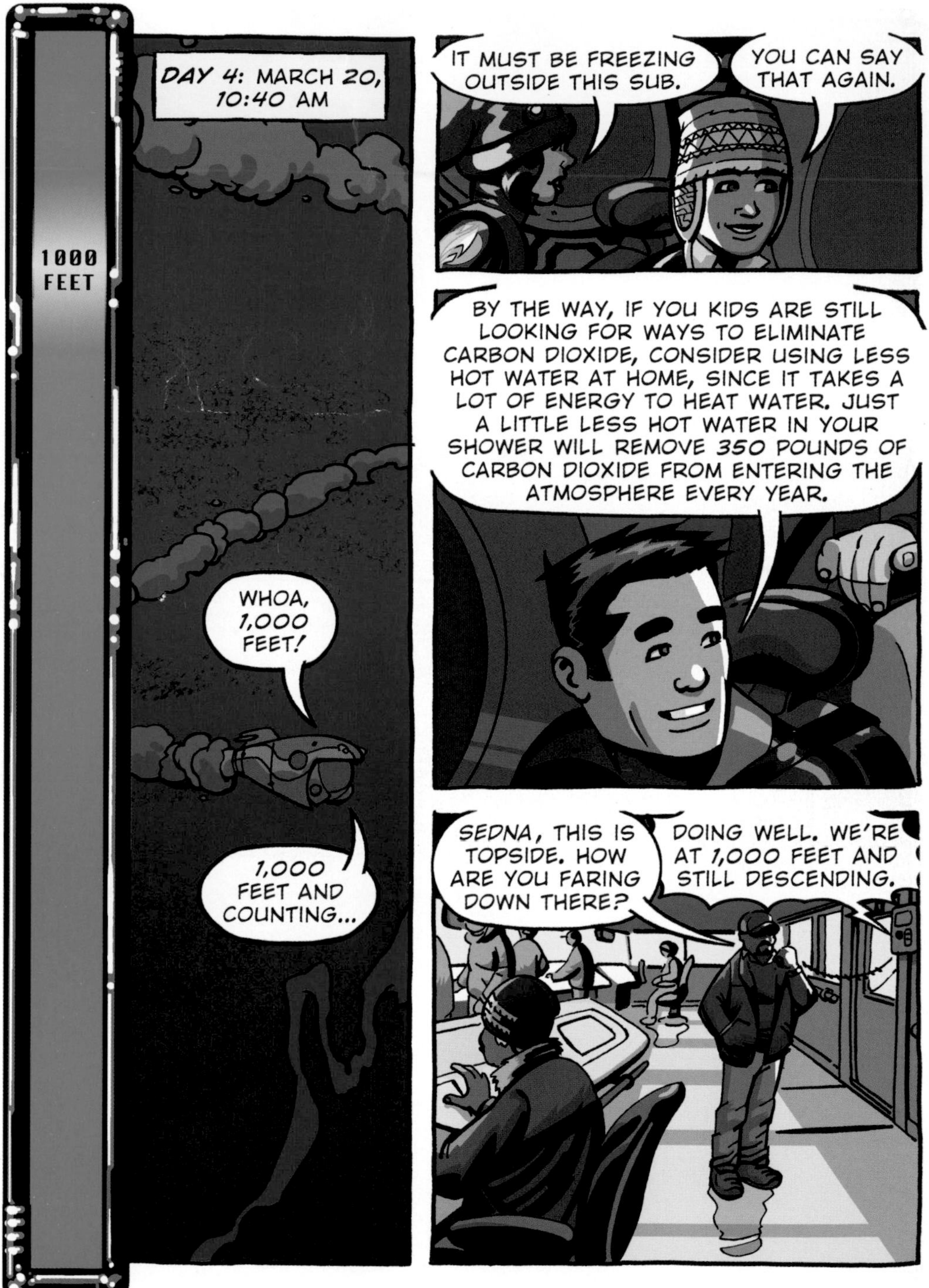

1000 FEET
DAY 4: MARCH 20, 10:40 AM
IT MUST BE FREEZING OUTSIDE THIS SUB.
YOU CAN SAY THAT AGAIN.
BY THE WAY, IF YOU KIDS ARE STILL LOOKING FOR WAYS TO ELIMINATE CARBON DIOXIDE, CONSIDER USING LESS HOT WATER AT HOME, SINCE IT TAKES A LOT OF ENERGY TO HEAT WATER. JUST A LITTLE LESS HOT WATER IN YOUR SHOWER WILL REMOVE 350 POUNDS OF CARBON DIOXIDE FROM ENTERING THE ATMOSPHERE EVERY YEAR.
WHOA, 1,000 FEET!
1,000 FEET AND COUNTING...
SEDNA, THIS IS TOPSIDE. HOW ARE YOU FARING DOWN THERE?
DOING WELL. WE'RE AT 1,000 FEET AND STILL DESCENDING.

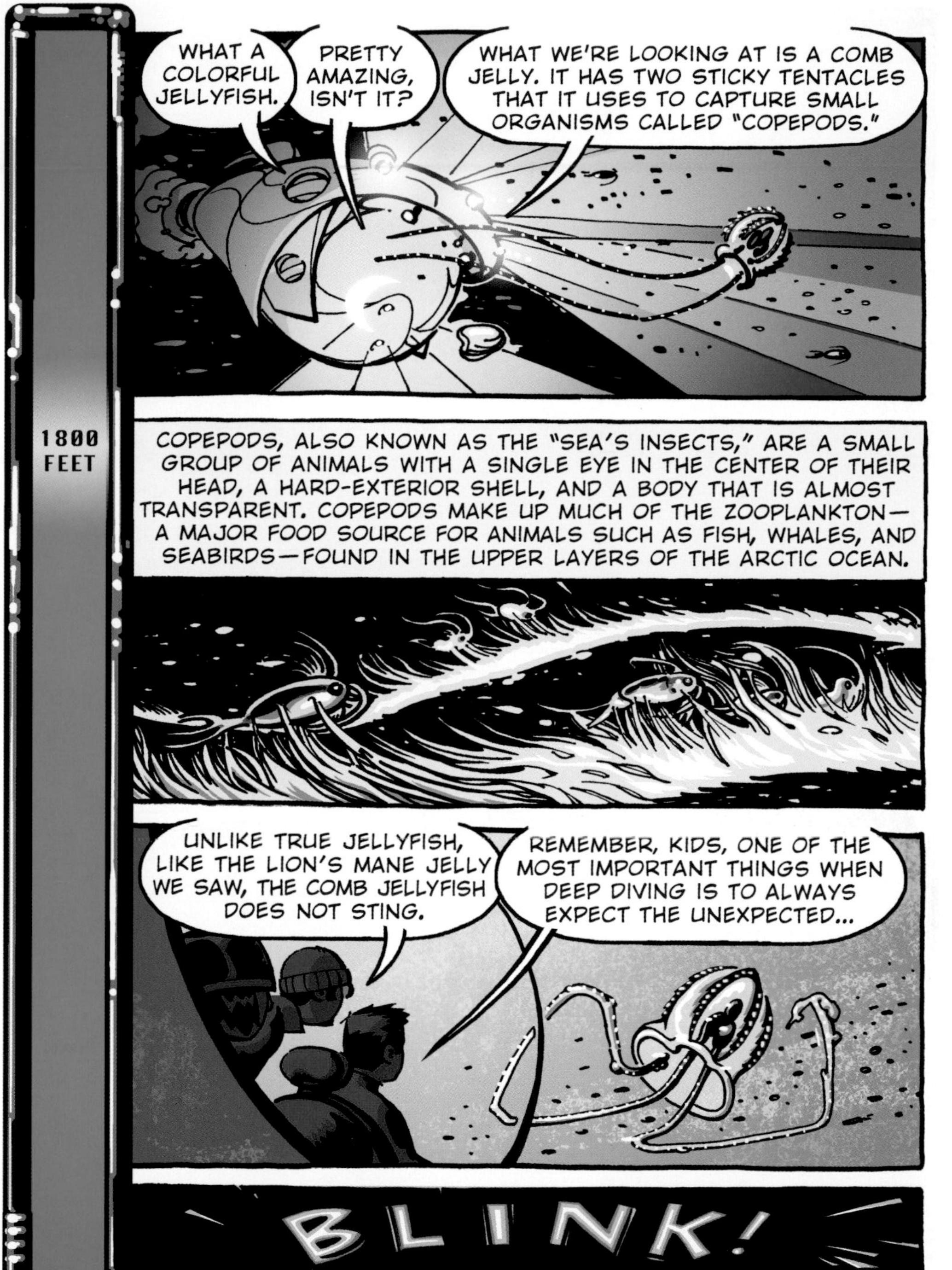
1800 FEET
WHAT A COLORFUL JELLYFISH.
PRETTY AMAZING, ISN'T IT?
WHAT WE'RE LOOKING AT IS A COMB JELLY. IT HAS TWO STICKY TENTACLES THAT IT USES TO CAPTURE SMALL ORGANISMS CALLED "COPEPODS."
COPEPODS, ALSO KNOWN AS THE "SEA'S INSECTS," ARE A SMALL GROUP OF ANIMALS WITH A SINGLE EYE IN THE CENTER OF THEIR HEAD, A HARD-EXTERIOR SHELL, AND A BODY THAT IS ALMOST TRANSPARENT. COPEPODS MAKE UP MUCH OF THE ZOOPLANKTON—A MAJOR FOOD SOURCE FOR ANIMALS SUCH AS FISH, WHALES, AND SEABIRDS—FOUND IN THE UPPER LAYERS OF THE ARCTIC OCEAN.
UNLIKE TRUE JELLYFISH, LIKE THE LION'S MANE JELLY WE SAW, THE COMB JELLYFISH DOES NOT STING.
REMEMBER, KIDS, ONE OF THE MOST IMPORTANT THINGS WHEN DEEP DIVING IS TO ALWAYS EXPECT THE UNEXPECTED...
BLINK!

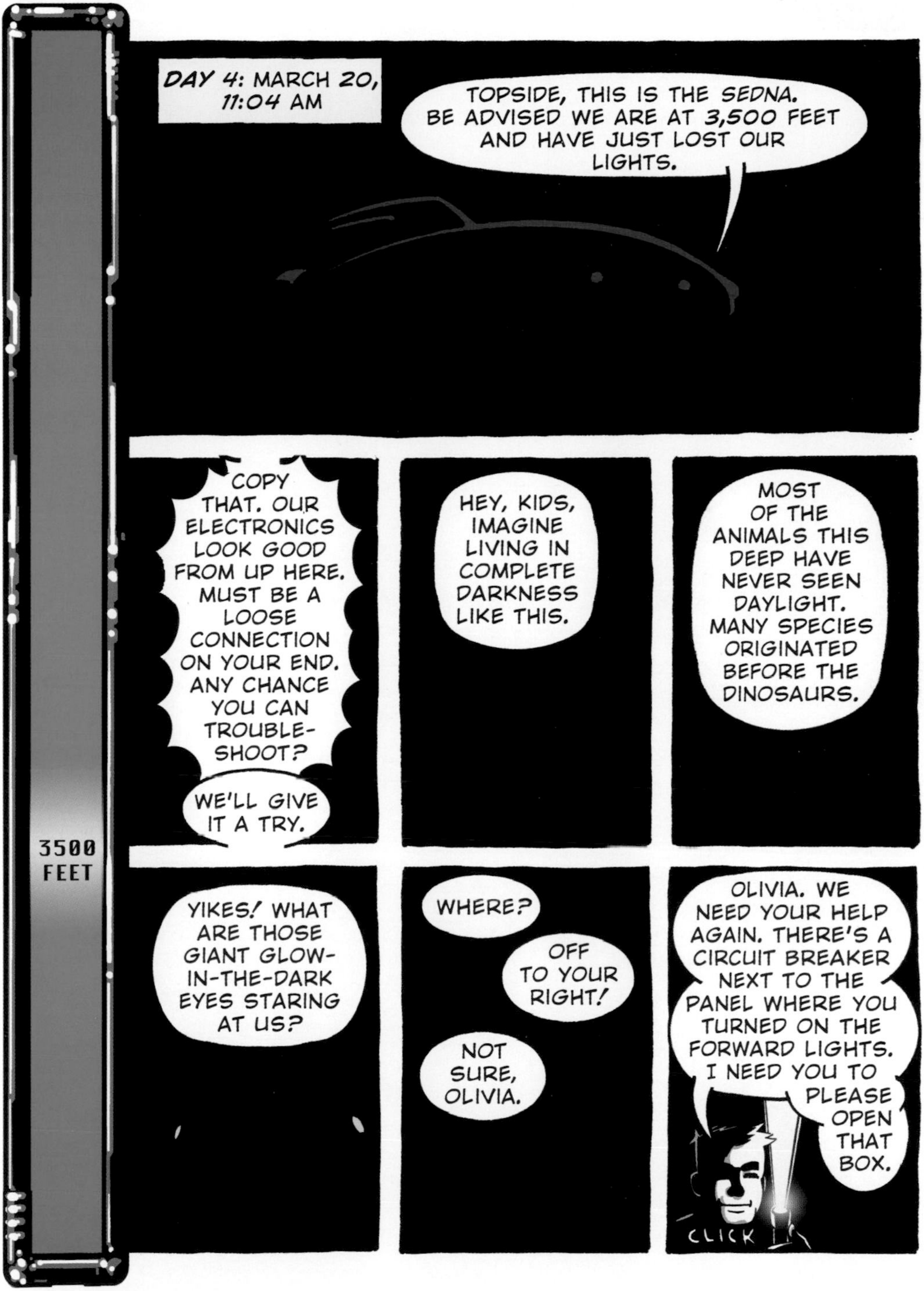
3500 FEET
DAY 4: MARCH 20, 11:04 AM
TOPSIDE, THIS IS THE SEDNA. BE ADVISED WE ARE AT 3,500 FEET AND HAVE JUST LOST OUR LIGHTS.
COPY THAT. OUR ELECTRONICS LOOK GOOD FROM UP HERE. MUST BE A LOOSE CONNECTION ON YOUR END. ANY CHANCE YOU CAN TROUBLE-SHOOT?
WE'LL GIVE IT A TRY.
HEY, KIDS, IMAGINE LIVING IN COMPLETE DARKNESS LIKE THIS.
MOST OF THE ANIMALS THIS DEEP HAVE NEVER SEEN DAYLIGHT. MANY SPECIES ORIGINATED BEFORE THE DINOSAURS.
YIKES! WHAT ARE THOSE GIANT GLOW-IN-THE-DARK EYES STARING AT US?
WHERE?
OFF TO YOUR RIGHT!
NOT SURE, OLIVIA.
OLIVIA. WE NEED YOUR HELP AGAIN. THERE'S A CIRCUIT BREAKER NEXT TO THE PANEL WHERE YOU TURNED ON THE FORWARD LIGHTS. I NEED YOU TO PLEASE OPEN THAT BOX.
CLICK

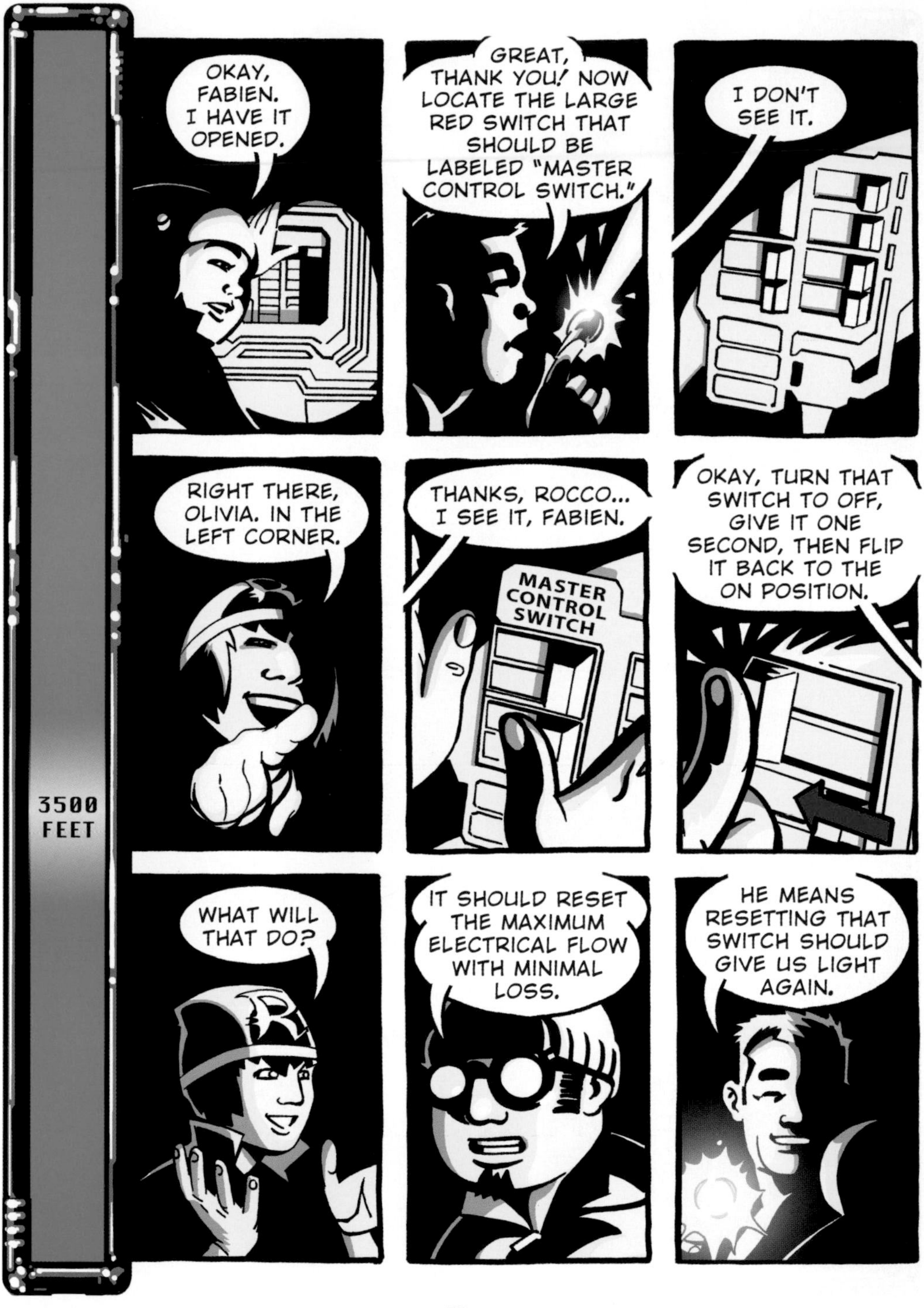
3500 FEET
OKAY, FABIEN. I HAVE IT OPENED.
GREAT, THANK YOU! NOW LOCATE THE LARGE RED SWITCH THAT SHOULD BE LABELED "MASTER CONTROL SWITCH."
I DON'T SEE IT.
RIGHT THERE, OLIVIA. IN THE LEFT CORNER.
THANKS, ROCCO... I SEE IT, FABIEN.
MASTER CONTROL SWITCH
OKAY, TURN THAT SWITCH TO OFF, GIVE IT ONE SECOND, THEN FLIP IT BACK TO THE ON POSITION.
WHAT WILL THAT DO?
IT SHOULD RESET THE MAXIMUM ELECTRICAL FLOW WITH MINIMAL LOSS.
HE MEANS RESETTING THAT SWITCH SHOULD GIVE US LIGHT AGAIN.

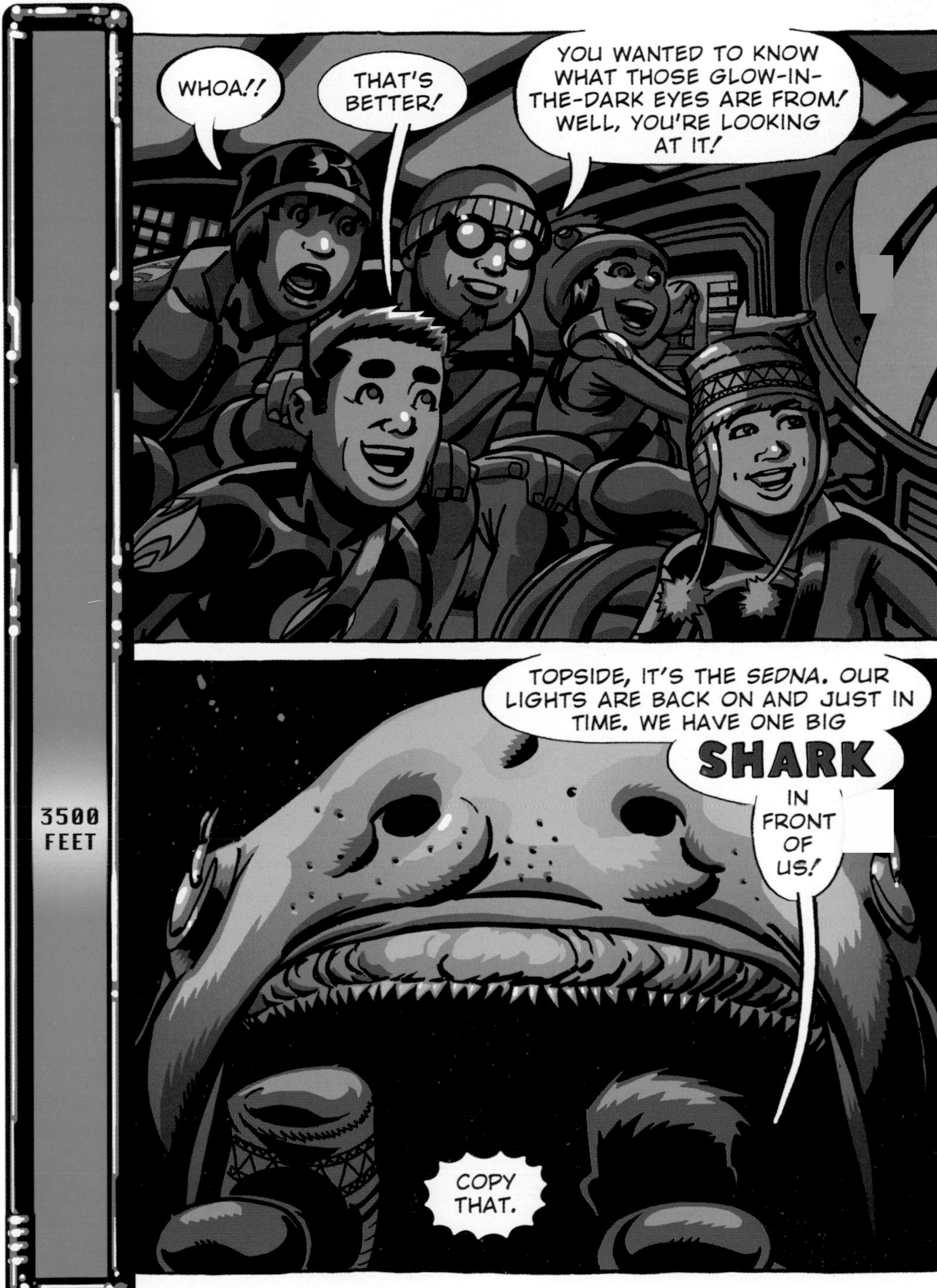

3500
FEET

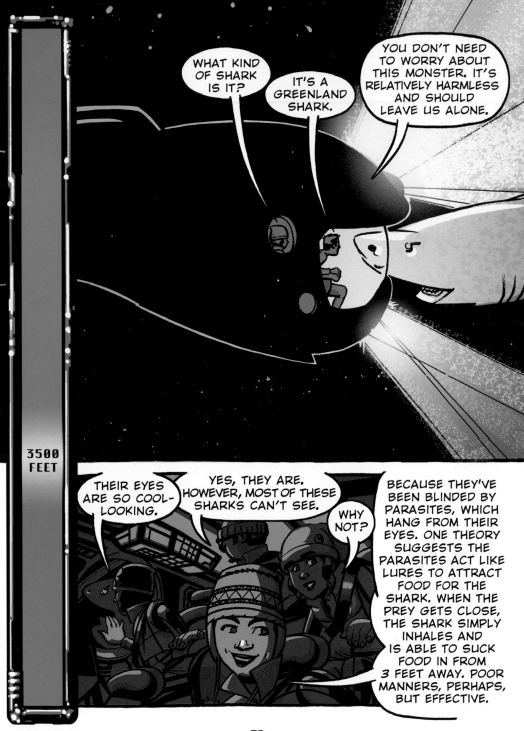

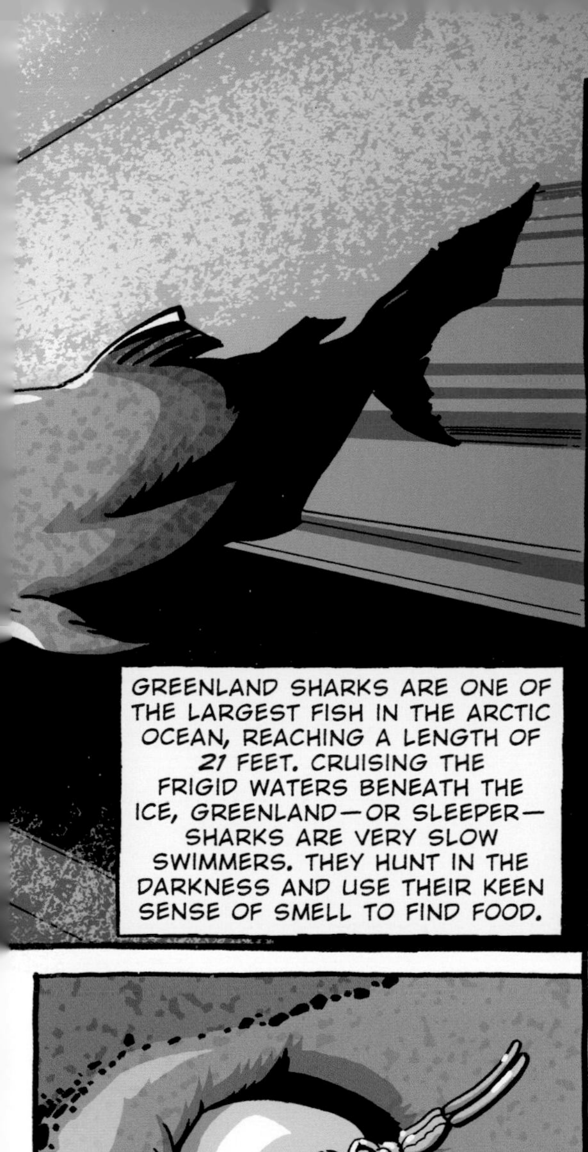
GREENLAND SHARKS ARE ONE OF THE LARGEST FISH IN THE ARCTIC OCEAN, REACHING A LENGTH OF 21 FEET. CRUISING THE FRIGID WATERS BENEATH THE ICE, GREENLAND—OR SLEEPER—SHARKS ARE VERY SLOW SWIMMERS. THEY HUNT IN THE DARKNESS AND USE THEIR KEEN SENSE OF SMELL TO FIND FOOD.

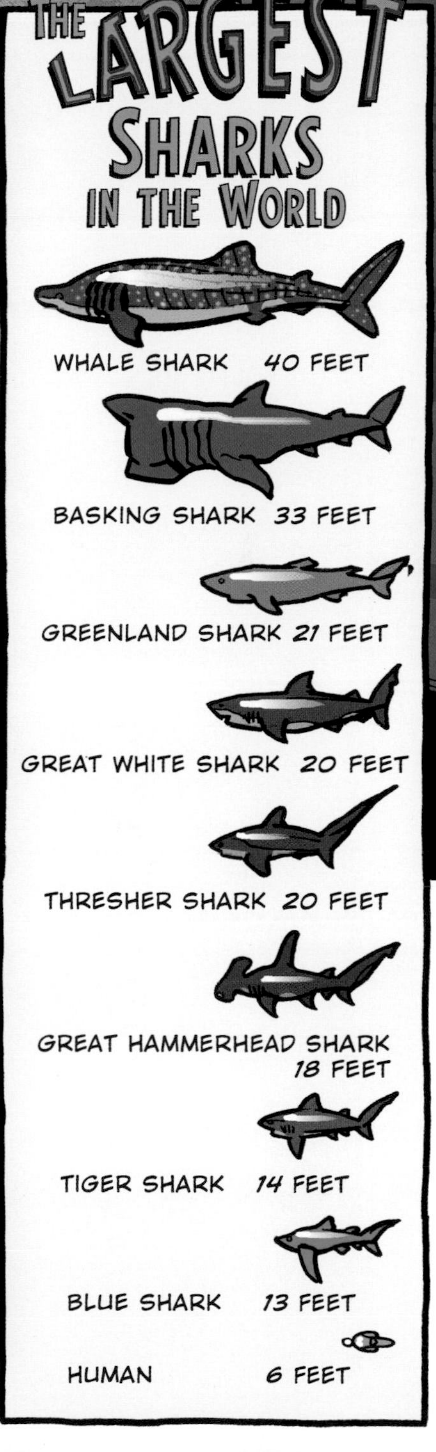
THE LARGEST SHARKS IN THE WORLD
WHALE SHARK 40 FEET
BASKING SHARK 33 FEET
GREENLAND SHARK 21 FEET
GREAT WHITE SHARK 20 FEET
THRESHER SHARK 20 FEET
GREAT HAMMERHEAD SHARK 18 FEET
TIGER SHARK 14 FEET
BLUE SHARK 13 FEET
HUMAN 6 FEET

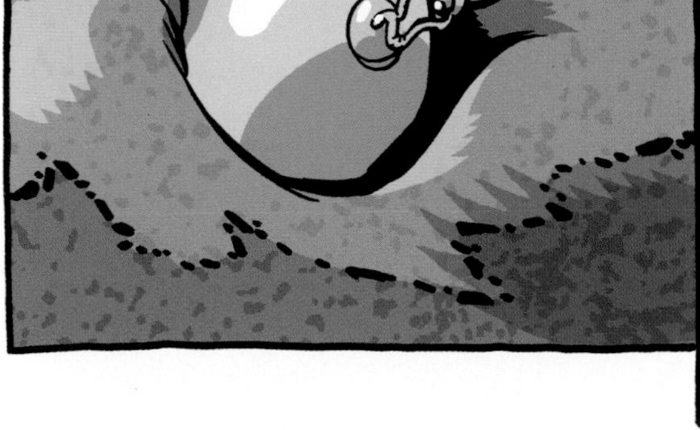

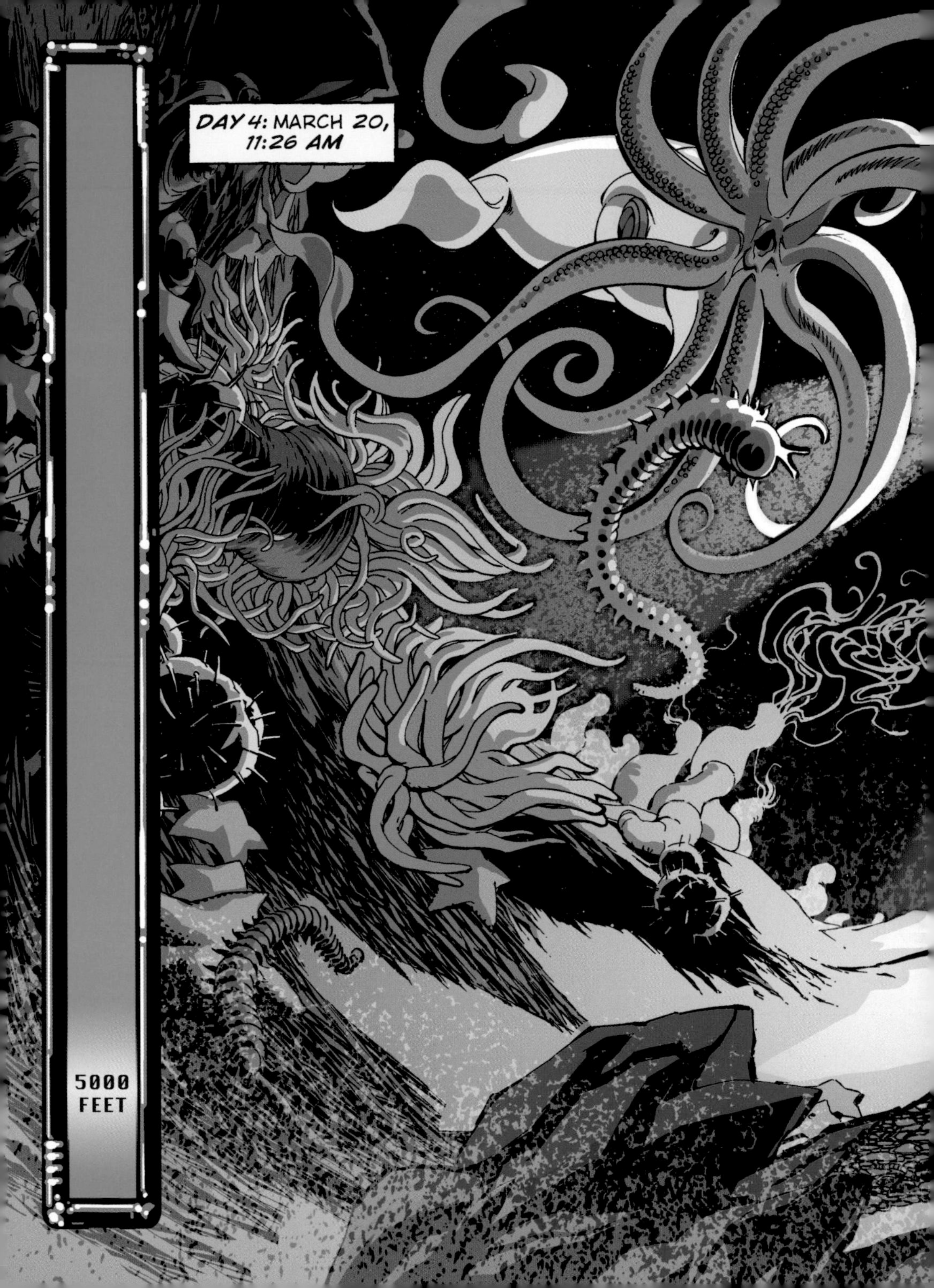
DAY 4: MARCH 20, 11:26 AM
5000 FEET

VERY COOL, AND FROM WHAT I CAN SEE, THERE'S QUITE A BIT OF LIFE DOWN HERE!

THERE SURE IS! INCLUDING THAT CURIOUS-LOOKING ARMHOOK SQUID AND A SNAILFISH.

ARMHOOK SQUID ARE A COMMON, MEDIUM-SIZE SQUID FOUND IN THE COLD WATERS OF THE ARCTIC OCEAN. THEY'RE CALLED "ARMHOOKS" BECAUSE THE FEMALES HAVE TENTACLES WITH SHARP HOOKS THAT HAVE REPLACED THE SUCTION CUPS SEEN ON OTHER SQUID.

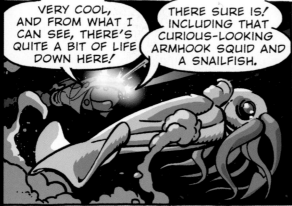

SNAILFISH ARE STRANGE-LOOKING CREATURES THAT HAVE A LARGE HEAD, SMALL EYES, AND A PINK BODY THAT NARROWS TO A VERY SMALL TAIL. THEY DO NOT HAVE SCALES, BUT INSTEAD ARE COVERED WITH A LOOSE, GELATINOUS SKIN.

CHECK OUT THOSE STARFISH. THEY LOOK DIFFERENT FROM THE ONES I'M USED TO SEEING BACK HOME.

THAT ONE WITH THE STUBBY LEGS IS AN ARCTIC COOKIE STAR. THE OTHER IS AN ARCTIC SEA STAR.

THESE ANIMALS CAN LOSE ONE OR MORE ARMS AND GROW NEW ONES, WHILE THEIR TUBE FEET ALLOW THEM TO CREEP IN ANY DIRECTION AND CLING TO STEEP SURFACES.

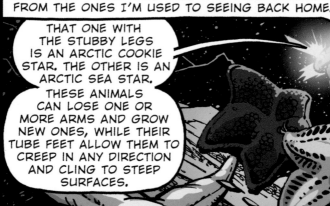

5018 FEET

5022 FEET

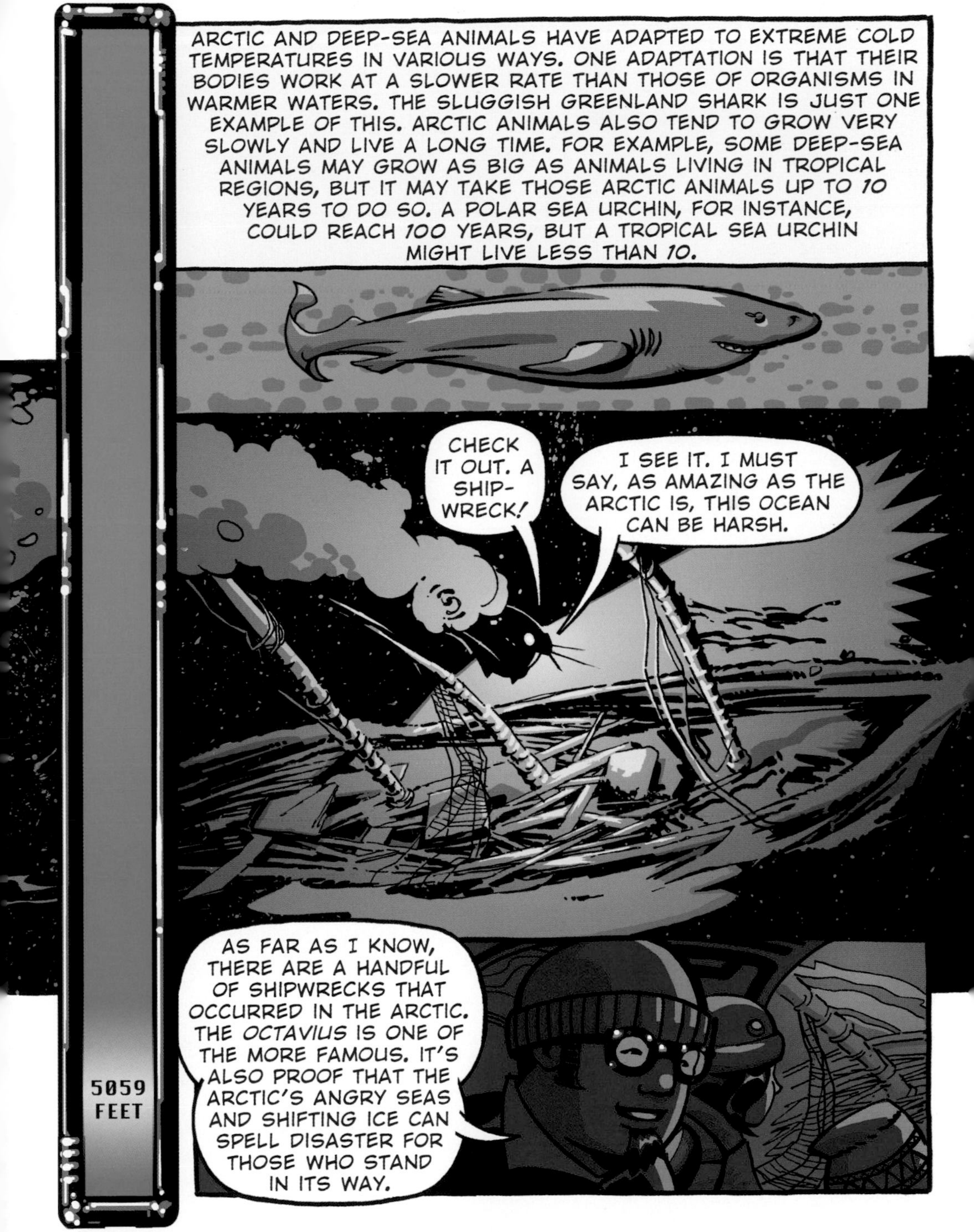
ARCTIC AND DEEP-SEA ANIMALS HAVE ADAPTED TO EXTREME COLD TEMPERATURES IN VARIOUS WAYS. ONE ADAPTATION IS THAT THEIR BODIES WORK AT A SLOWER RATE THAN THOSE OF ORGANISMS IN WARMER WATERS. THE SLUGGISH GREENLAND SHARK IS JUST ONE EXAMPLE OF THIS. ARCTIC ANIMALS ALSO TEND TO GROW VERY SLOWLY AND LIVE A LONG TIME. FOR EXAMPLE, SOME DEEP-SEA ANIMALS MAY GROW AS BIG AS ANIMALS LIVING IN TROPICAL REGIONS, BUT IT MAY TAKE THOSE ARCTIC ANIMALS UP TO 10 YEARS TO DO SO. A POLAR SEA URCHIN, FOR INSTANCE, COULD REACH 100 YEARS, BUT A TROPICAL SEA URCHIN MIGHT LIVE LESS THAN 10.
CHECK IT OUT. A SHIPWRECK!
I SEE IT. I MUST SAY, AS AMAZING AS THE ARCTIC IS, THIS OCEAN CAN BE HARSH.
AS FAR AS I KNOW, THERE ARE A HANDFUL OF SHIPWRECKS THAT OCCURRED IN THE ARCTIC. THE *OCTAVIUS* IS ONE OF THE MORE FAMOUS. IT'S ALSO PROOF THAT THE ARCTIC'S ANGRY SEAS AND SHIFTING ICE CAN SPELL DISASTER FOR THOSE WHO STAND IN ITS WAY.
5059 FEET

WHAT IS THE *OCTAVIUS*, MATT?

IT WAS AN ENGLISH TRADING SHIP THAT SAILED THE ARCTIC OCEAN IN *1775*. ACCORDING TO LEGEND, THE CAPTAIN OF A WHALING SHIP CAME UPON THE VESSEL YEARS LATER, TRAPPED IN THE SEA ICE.

WHAT DID HE FIND?

APPARENTLY, A VERY CHILLING SIGHT. THERE, SLUMPED OVER HIS TABLE, FROZEN TO DEATH, WAS THE CAPTAIN OF THE *OCTAVIUS*. HIS CREW WAS ALSO FROZEN, STILL HUDDLED IN BLANKETS IN THEIR BUNKS.

CREEPY!

THE UNITED NATIONS ESTIMATES THERE ARE MORE THAN 3 MILLION SHIPWRECKS RESTING ON THE SEA FLOOR.

SEEMS THE COMPASS NEEDLE IS POINTING IN THE DIRECTION OF A LARGE, DARK SHADOW IN THE DISTANCE.

HEY, MAYBE THAT'S OUR CAVE!

YOU COULD BE RIGHT, OLIVIA. LET'S GO HAVE A LOOK!

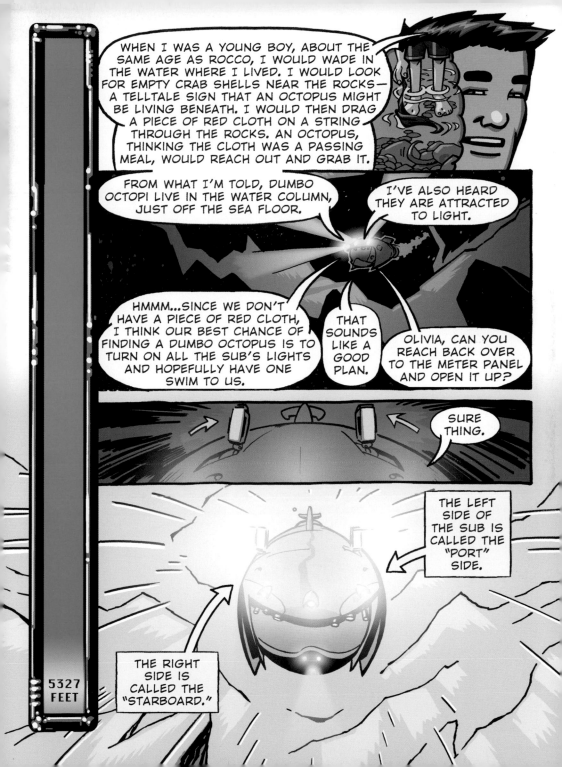

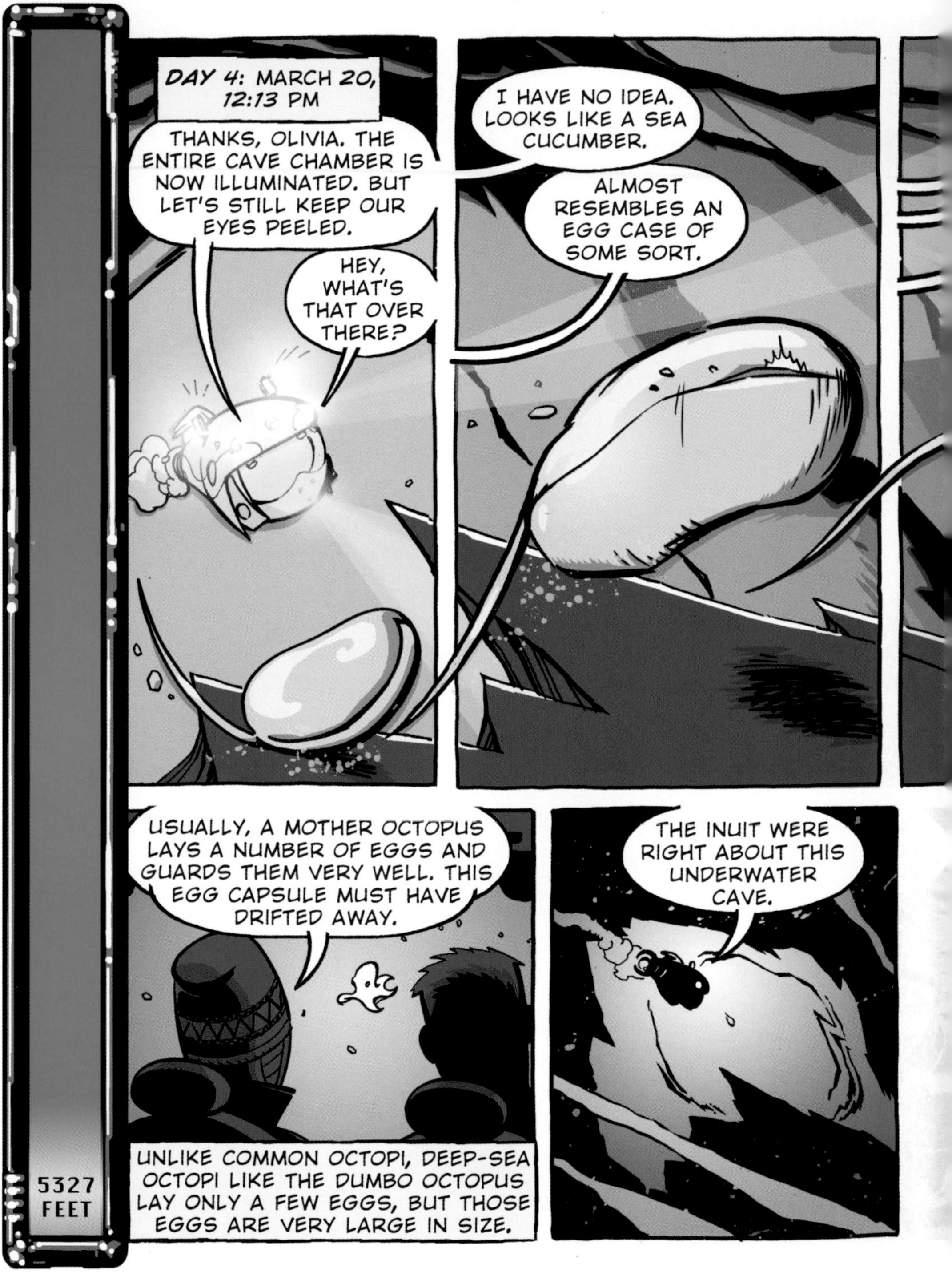
DAY 4: MARCH 20, 12:13 PM
THANKS, OLIVIA. THE ENTIRE CAVE CHAMBER IS NOW ILLUMINATED. BUT LET'S STILL KEEP OUR EYES PEELED.
HEY, WHAT'S THAT OVER THERE?
I HAVE NO IDEA. LOOKS LIKE A SEA CUCUMBER.
ALMOST RESEMBLES AN EGG CASE OF SOME SORT.
USUALLY, A MOTHER OCTOPUS LAYS A NUMBER OF EGGS AND GUARDS THEM VERY WELL. THIS EGG CAPSULE MUST HAVE DRIFTED AWAY.
UNLIKE COMMON OCTOPI, DEEP-SEA OCTOPI LIKE THE DUMBO OCTOPUS LAY ONLY A FEW EGGS, BUT THOSE EGGS ARE VERY LARGE IN SIZE.
THE INUIT WERE RIGHT ABOUT THIS UNDERWATER CAVE.
5327 FEET

85

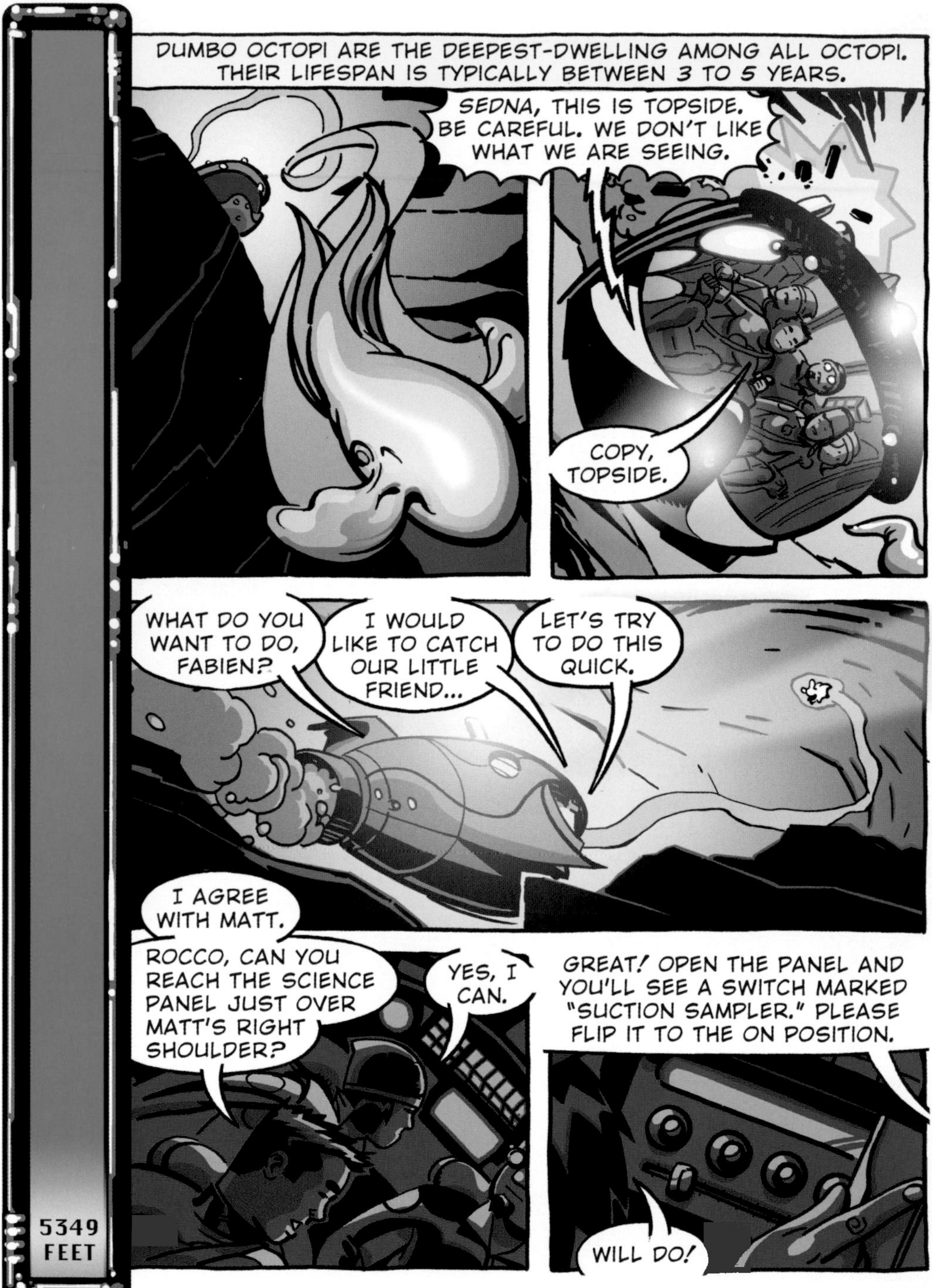
DUMBO OCTOPI ARE THE DEEPEST-DWELLING AMONG ALL OCTOPI. THEIR LIFESPAN IS TYPICALLY BETWEEN 3 TO 5 YEARS.
SEDNA, THIS IS TOPSIDE. BE CAREFUL. WE DON'T LIKE WHAT WE ARE SEEING.
COPY, TOPSIDE.
WHAT DO YOU WANT TO DO, FABIEN?
I WOULD LIKE TO CATCH OUR LITTLE FRIEND...
LET'S TRY TO DO THIS QUICK.
I AGREE WITH MATT.
ROCCO, CAN YOU REACH THE SCIENCE PANEL JUST OVER MATT'S RIGHT SHOULDER?
YES, I CAN.
GREAT! OPEN THE PANEL AND YOU'LL SEE A SWITCH MARKED "SUCTION SAMPLER." PLEASE FLIP IT TO THE ON POSITION.
WILL DO!
5349 FEET

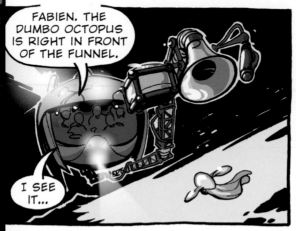

FABIEN. THE DUMBO OCTOPUS IS RIGHT IN FRONT OF THE FUNNEL.

I SEE IT...

FABIEN, YOU MIGHT WANT TO REDUCE THE SUCTION'S PRESSURE SO THE OCTOPUS WILL DRIFT INSIDE RATHER THAN GET SLURPED UP.

GOOD THINKING, GLORIA...MATT, CAN YOU REACH THE PRESSURE VALVE?

YES, NO PROBLEM. I'LL LOWER THE PRESSURE TO MINIMAL SUCTION.

THE BABY OCTOPUS IS NOW INSIDE THE SUCTION TUBE.

ZIP

EXCELLENT WORK... I'M GOING TO REDUCE THE PRESSURE EVEN MORE SO THE OCTOPUS CAN ENTER THE COLLECTION BUCKET VERY SLOWLY. WE DON'T WANT TO INJURE IT.

THANKS, MATT.

TOPSIDE, IT'S THE SEDNA. WE ARE SERIOUSLY LOW ON POWER!

LOW POWER

5372 FEET

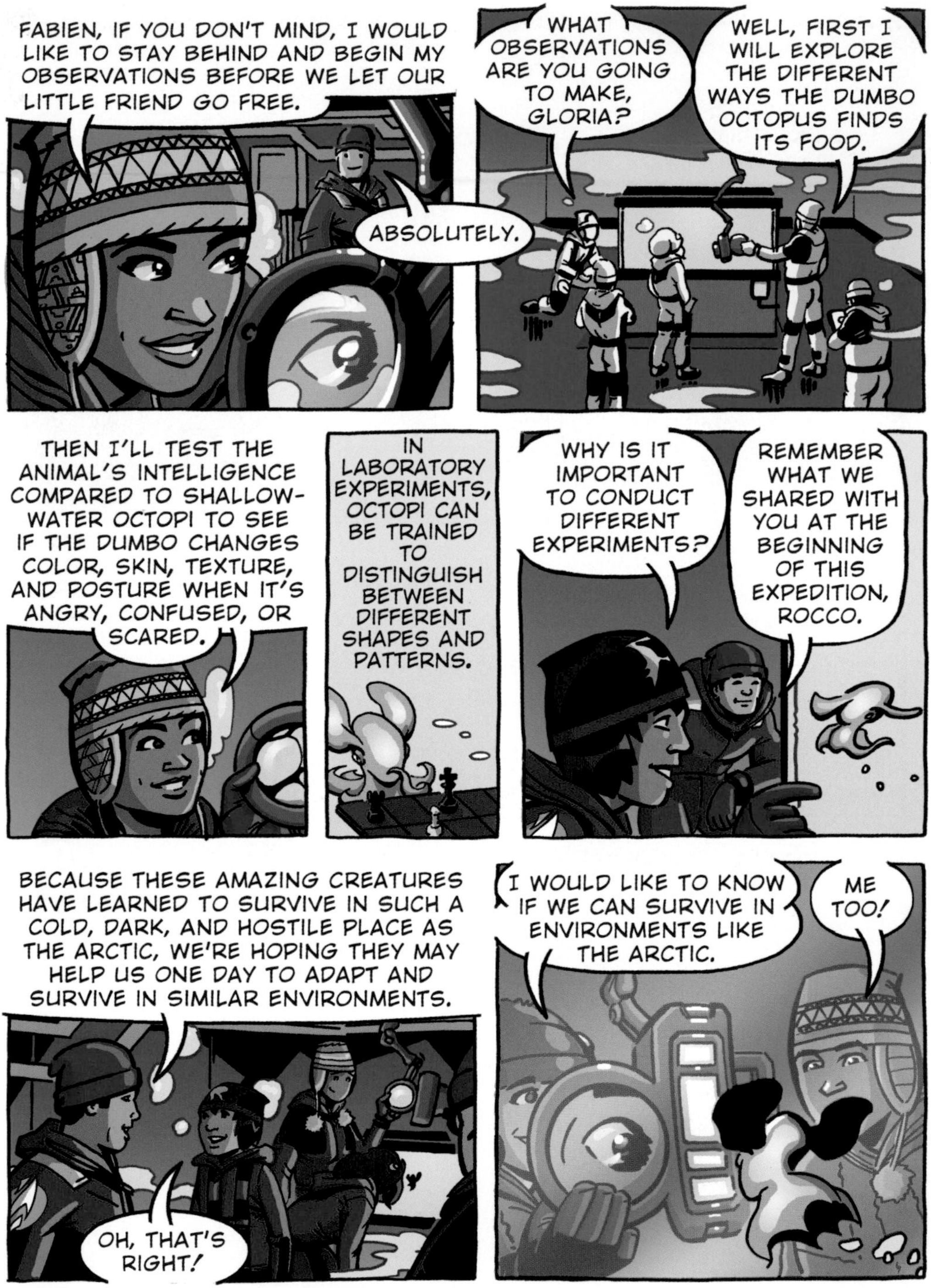
FABIEN, IF YOU DON'T MIND, I WOULD LIKE TO STAY BEHIND AND BEGIN MY OBSERVATIONS BEFORE WE LET OUR LITTLE FRIEND GO FREE.
ABSOLUTELY.
WHAT OBSERVATIONS ARE YOU GOING TO MAKE, GLORIA?
WELL, FIRST I WILL EXPLORE THE DIFFERENT WAYS THE DUMBO OCTOPUS FINDS ITS FOOD.
THEN I'LL TEST THE ANIMAL'S INTELLIGENCE COMPARED TO SHALLOW-WATER OCTOPI TO SEE IF THE DUMBO CHANGES COLOR, SKIN, TEXTURE, AND POSTURE WHEN IT'S ANGRY, CONFUSED, OR SCARED.
IN LABORATORY EXPERIMENTS, OCTOPI CAN BE TRAINED TO DISTINGUISH BETWEEN DIFFERENT SHAPES AND PATTERNS.
WHY IS IT IMPORTANT TO CONDUCT DIFFERENT EXPERIMENTS?
REMEMBER WHAT WE SHARED WITH YOU AT THE BEGINNING OF THIS EXPEDITION, ROCCO.
BECAUSE THESE AMAZING CREATURES HAVE LEARNED TO SURVIVE IN SUCH A COLD, DARK, AND HOSTILE PLACE AS THE ARCTIC, WE'RE HOPING THEY MAY HELP US ONE DAY TO ADAPT AND SURVIVE IN SIMILAR ENVIRONMENTS.
OH, THAT'S RIGHT!
I WOULD LIKE TO KNOW IF WE CAN SURVIVE IN ENVIRONMENTS LIKE THE ARCTIC.
ME TOO!

THE INUIT DRUM IS CALLED A *QILAUT* AND IS TRADITIONALLY MADE FROM CARIBOU SKIN WITH SEAL OR WALRUS SKIN AROUND THE HANDLE.

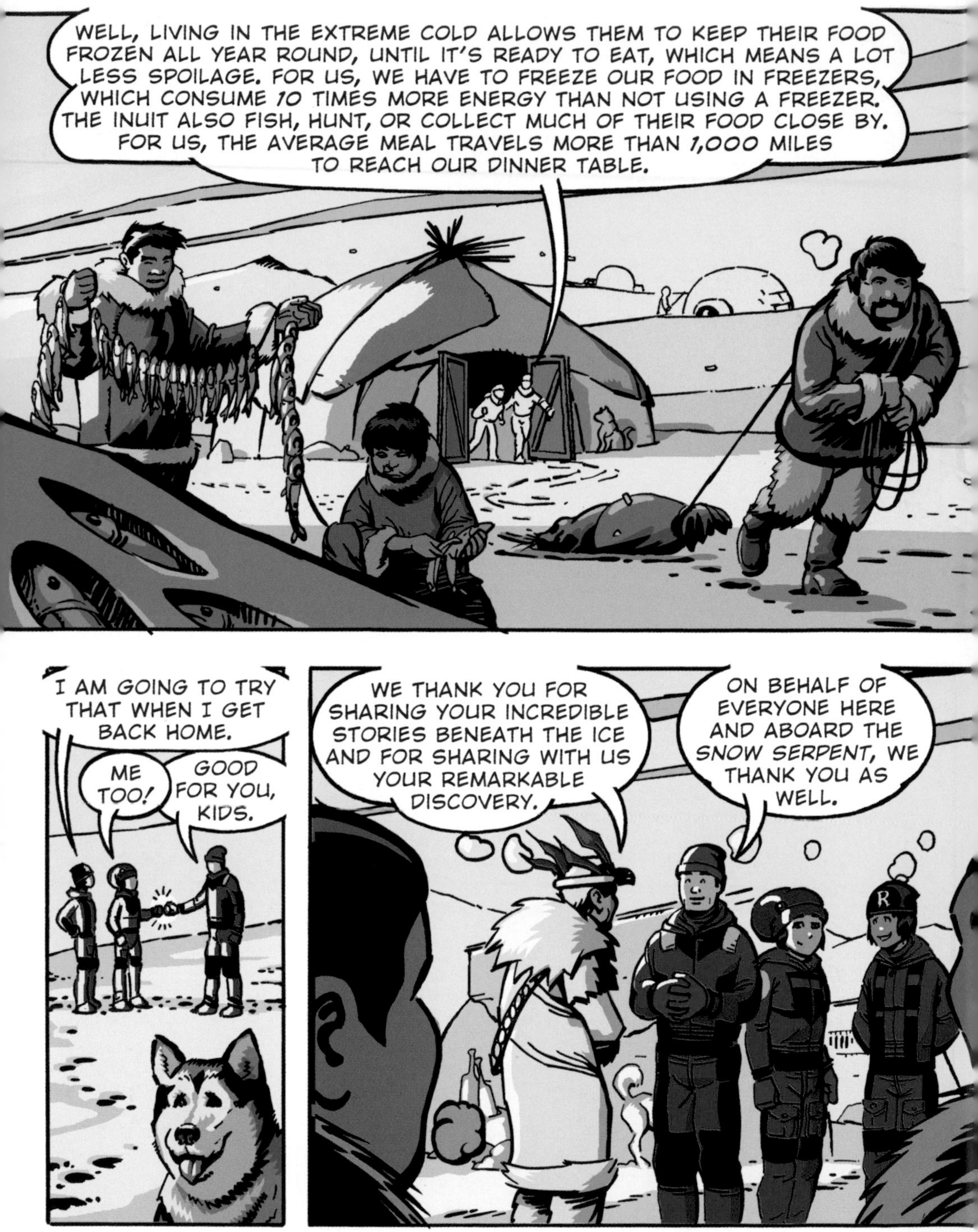
WELL, LIVING IN THE EXTREME COLD ALLOWS THEM TO KEEP THEIR FOOD FROZEN ALL YEAR ROUND, UNTIL IT'S READY TO EAT, WHICH MEANS A LOT LESS SPOILAGE. FOR US, WE HAVE TO FREEZE OUR FOOD IN FREEZERS, WHICH CONSUME *10* TIMES MORE ENERGY THAN NOT USING A FREEZER. THE INUIT ALSO FISH, HUNT, OR COLLECT MUCH OF THEIR FOOD CLOSE BY. FOR US, THE AVERAGE MEAL TRAVELS MORE THAN *1,000* MILES TO REACH OUR DINNER TABLE.
I AM GOING TO TRY THAT WHEN I GET BACK HOME.
ME TOO!
GOOD FOR YOU, KIDS.
WE THANK YOU FOR SHARING YOUR INCREDIBLE STORIES BENEATH THE ICE AND FOR SHARING WITH US YOUR REMARKABLE DISCOVERY.
ON BEHALF OF EVERYONE HERE AND ABOARD THE *SNOW SERPENT*, WE THANK YOU AS WELL.

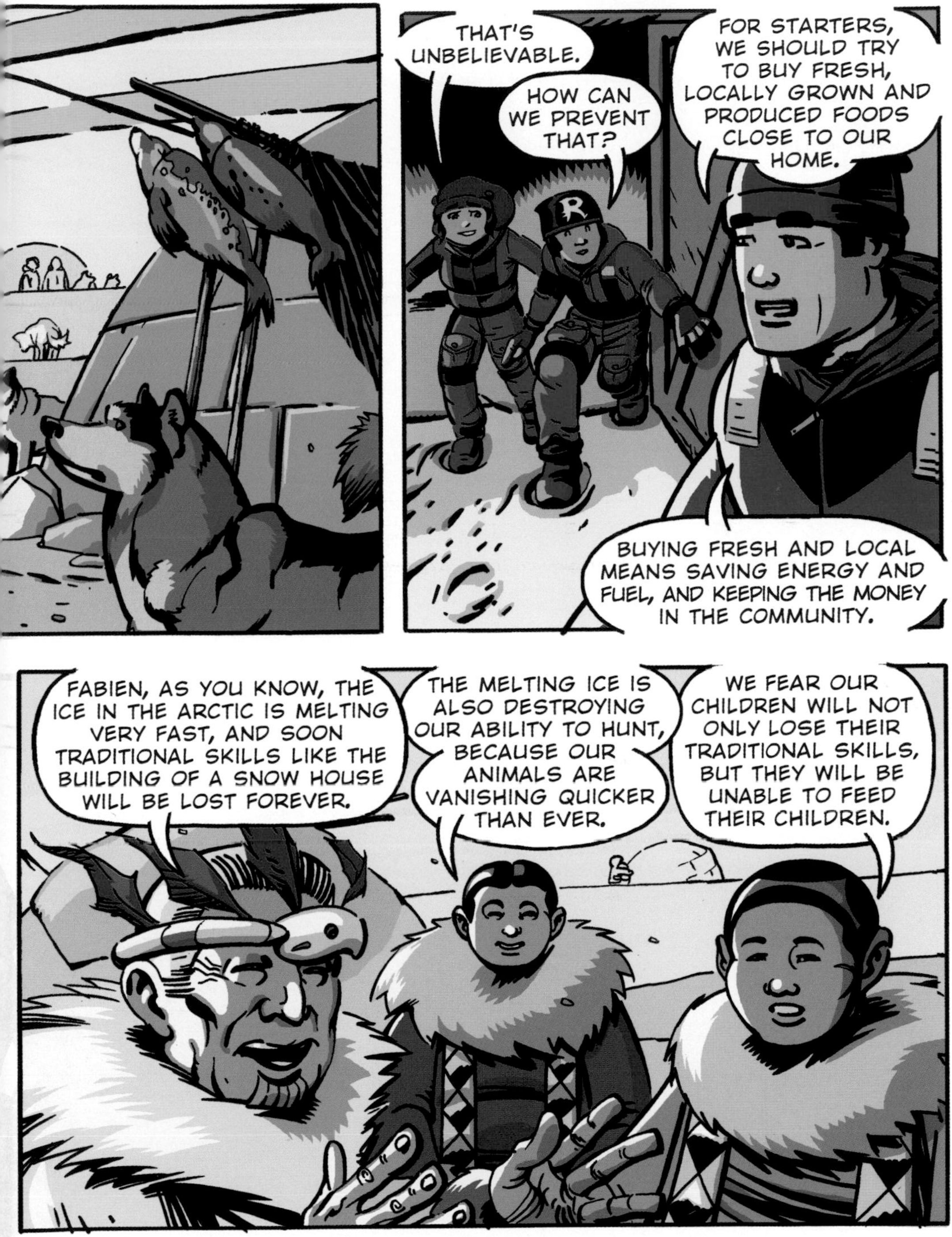
THAT'S UNBELIEVABLE.
HOW CAN WE PREVENT THAT?
FOR STARTERS, WE SHOULD TRY TO BUY FRESH, LOCALLY GROWN AND PRODUCED FOODS CLOSE TO OUR HOME.
BUYING FRESH AND LOCAL MEANS SAVING ENERGY AND FUEL, AND KEEPING THE MONEY IN THE COMMUNITY.
FABIEN, AS YOU KNOW, THE ICE IN THE ARCTIC IS MELTING VERY FAST, AND SOON TRADITIONAL SKILLS LIKE THE BUILDING OF A SNOW HOUSE WILL BE LOST FOREVER.
THE MELTING ICE IS ALSO DESTROYING OUR ABILITY TO HUNT, BECAUSE OUR ANIMALS ARE VANISHING QUICKER THAN EVER.
WE FEAR OUR CHILDREN WILL NOT ONLY LOSE THEIR TRADITIONAL SKILLS, BUT THEY WILL BE UNABLE TO FEED THEIR CHILDREN.

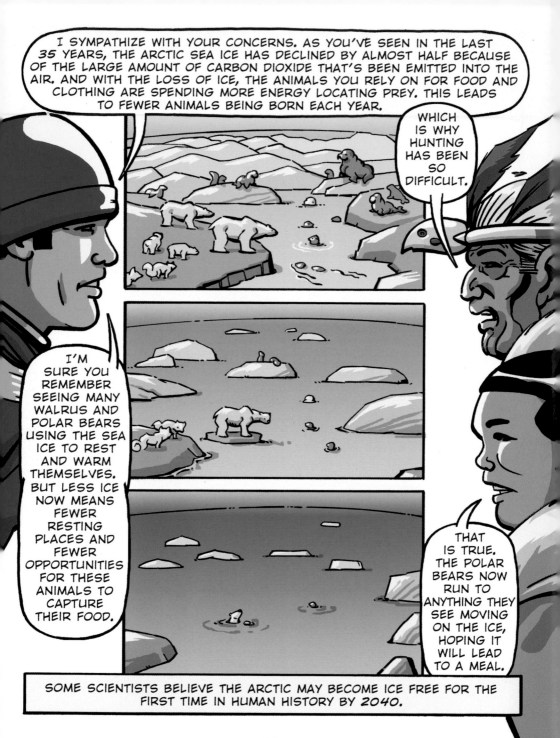

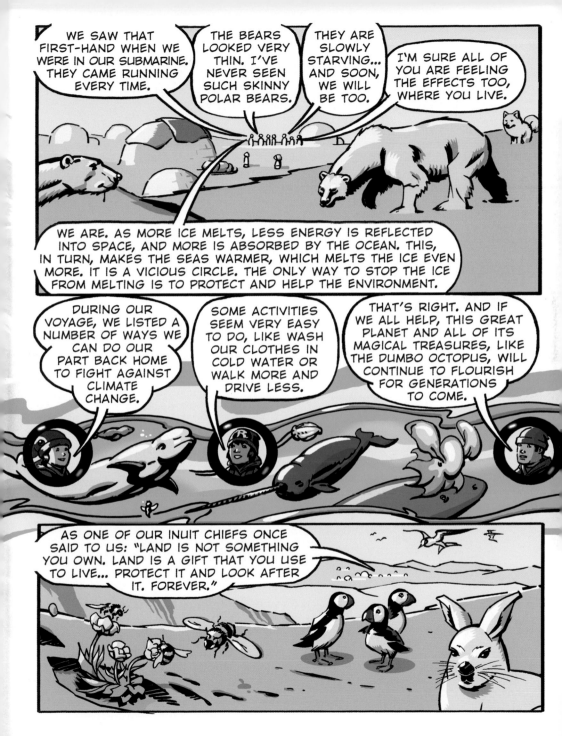

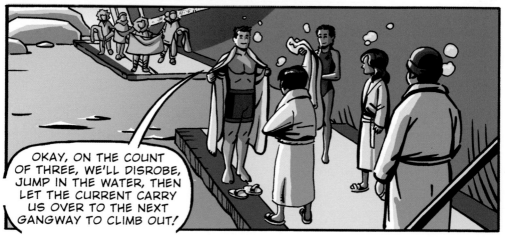

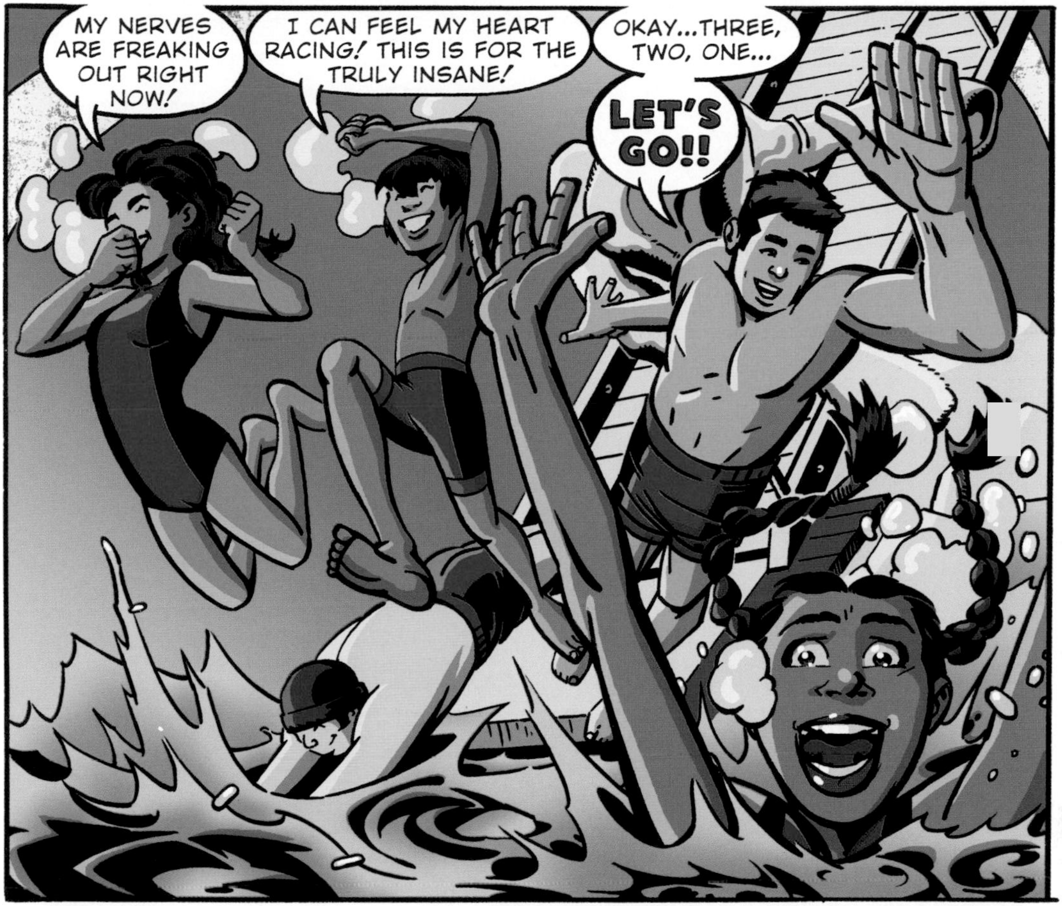
MY NERVES ARE FREAKING OUT RIGHT NOW!
I CAN FEEL MY HEART RACING! THIS IS FOR THE TRULY INSANE!
OKAY...THREE, TWO, ONE...
LET'S GO!!

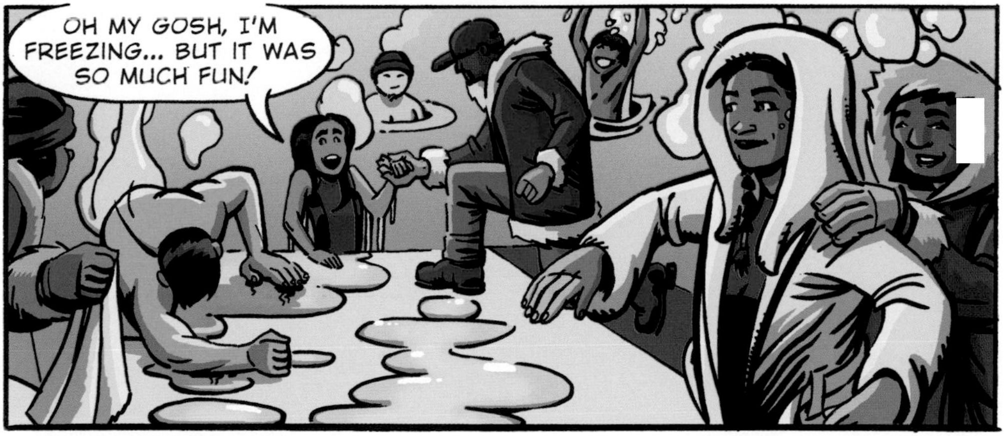
OH MY GOSH, I'M FREEZING... BUT IT WAS SO MUCH FUN!

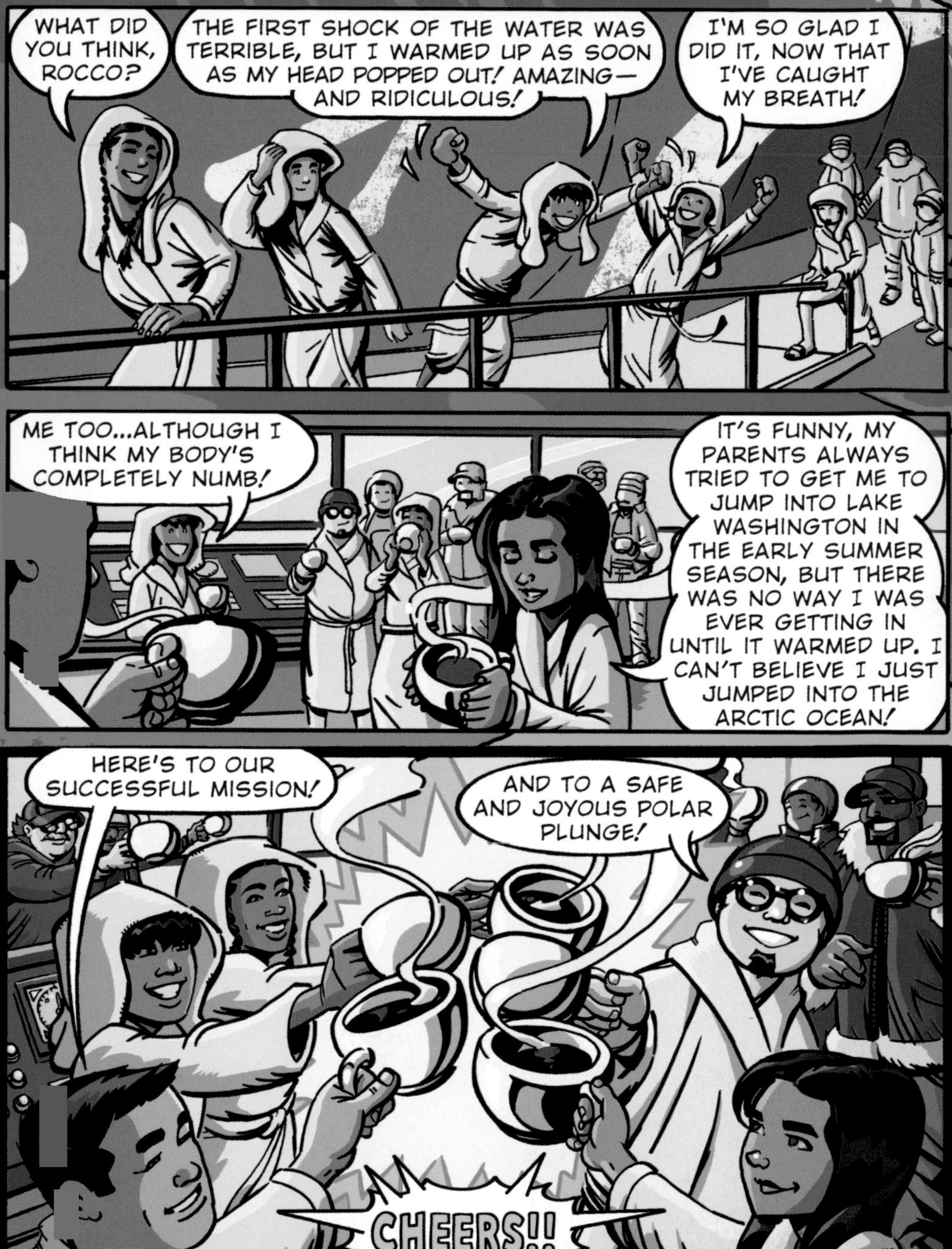
WHAT DID YOU THINK, ROCCO?
THE FIRST SHOCK OF THE WATER WAS TERRIBLE, BUT I WARMED UP AS SOON AS MY HEAD POPPED OUT! AMAZING— AND RIDICULOUS!
I'M SO GLAD I DID IT, NOW THAT I'VE CAUGHT MY BREATH!
ME TOO...ALTHOUGH I THINK MY BODY'S COMPLETELY NUMB!
IT'S FUNNY, MY PARENTS ALWAYS TRIED TO GET ME TO JUMP INTO LAKE WASHINGTON IN THE EARLY SUMMER SEASON, BUT THERE WAS NO WAY I WAS EVER GETTING IN UNTIL IT WARMED UP. I CAN'T BELIEVE I JUST JUMPED INTO THE ARCTIC OCEAN!
HERE'S TO OUR SUCCESSFUL MISSION!
AND TO A SAFE AND JOYOUS POLAR PLUNGE!
CHEERS!!

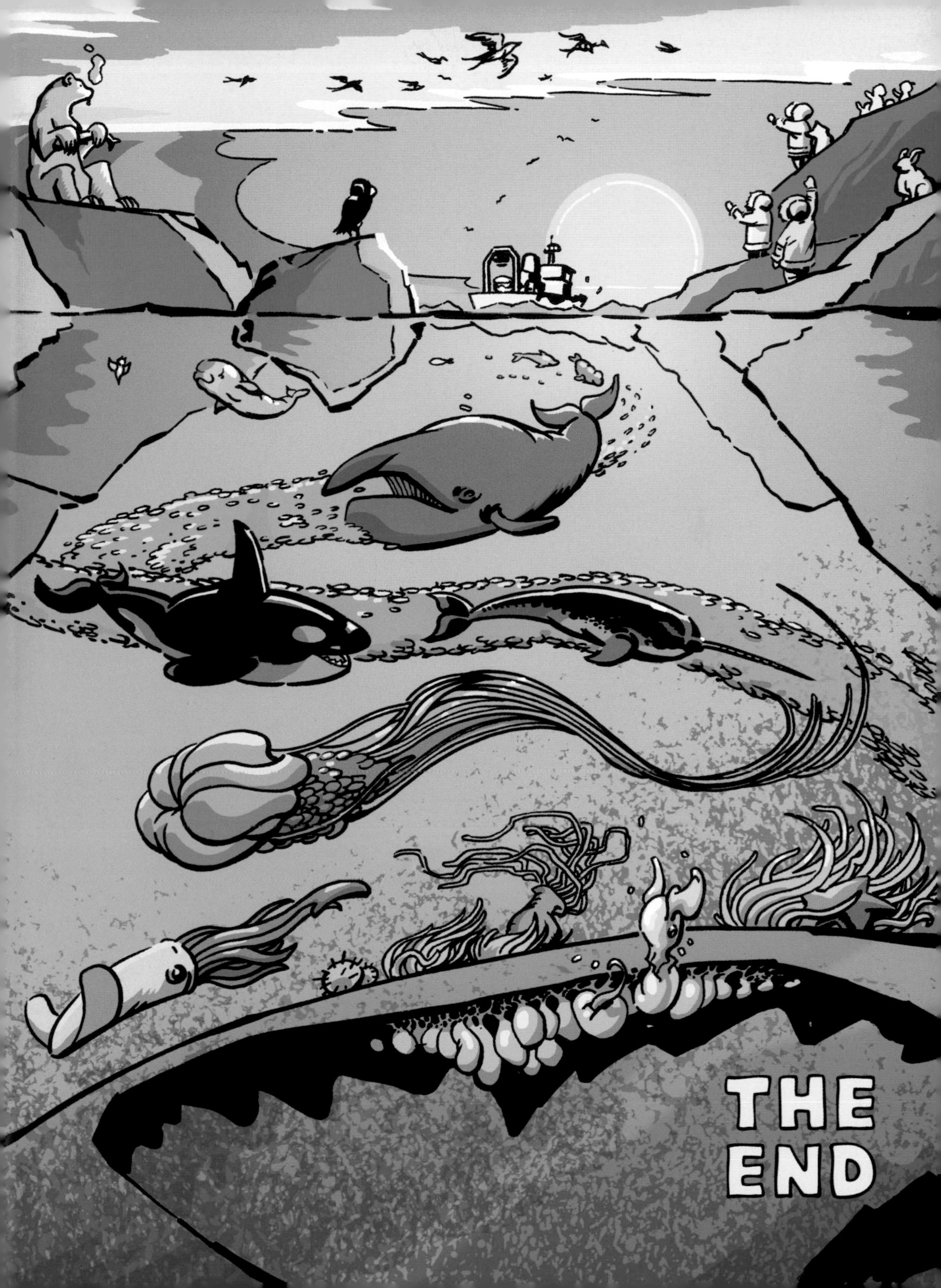
THE
END

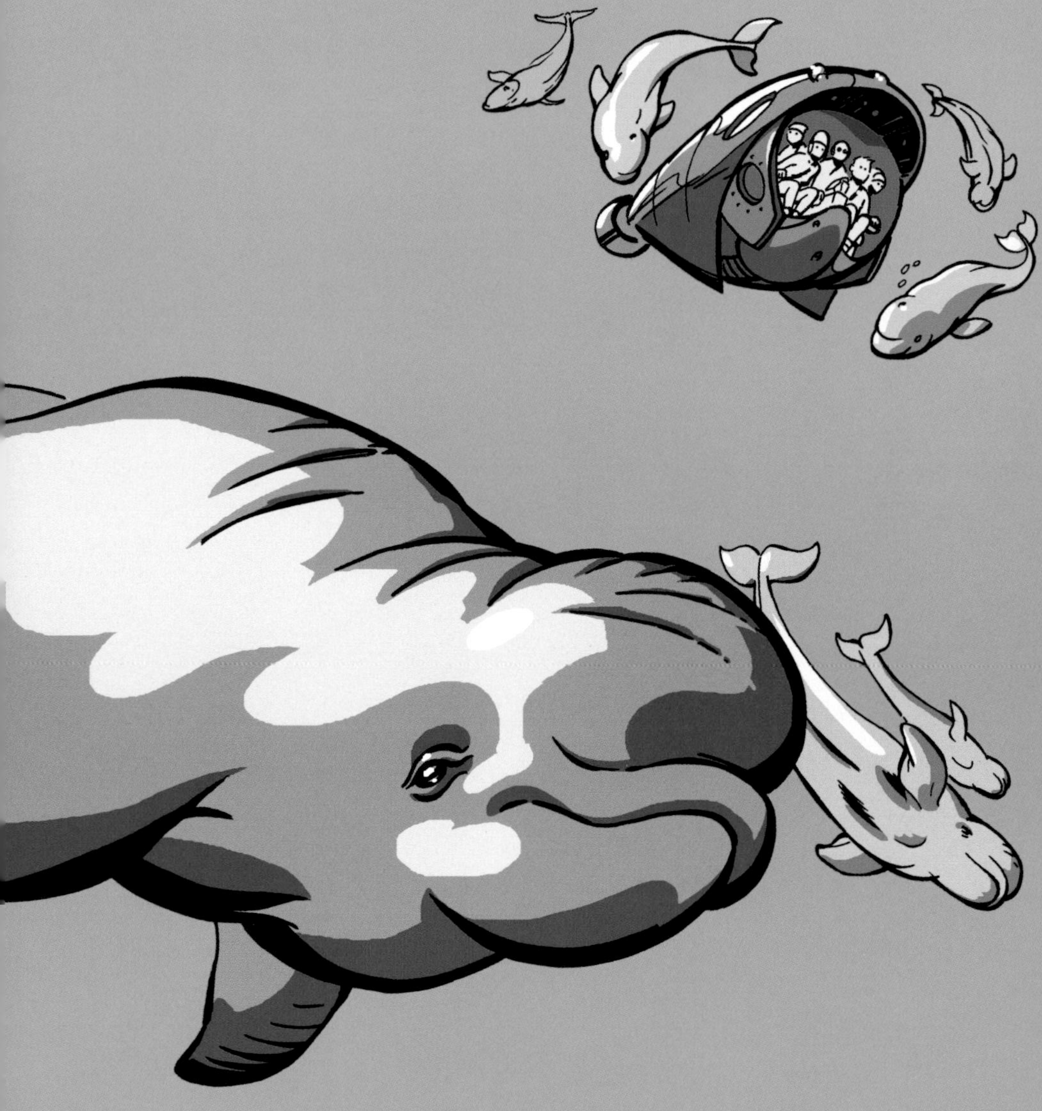

The author and artist would like to thank the wonderfully talented editorial-publishing team at Margaret K. McElderry Books and Simon & Schuster Children's Publishing, including Karen Wojtyla, Sonia Chaghatzbanian, Tom Daly, and Nicole Fiorica; Paul Zemitzsch and Explore Green; David Tanguay and Sonya Pelletier for their coloring assistance; and Professor Jean-Michel Huctin and the Research Centre CEARC from the University of Versailles Saint-Quentin-en-Yvelines, France, for his review of Inuit traditions and culture.

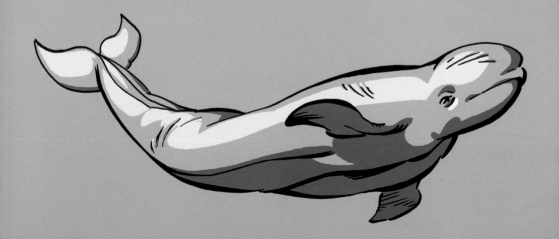

FABIEN COUSTEAU is the grandson of famed sea explorer Jacques Cousteau and a third generation ocean explorer and filmmaker. He has worked with National Geographic, Discovery, PBS, and CBS to produce ocean exploration documentaries, and continues to produce environmentally oriented content for schools, books, magazines, and newspapers. Learn more about his work at fabiencousteauolc.org.

JAMES O. FRAIOLI is a published author of twenty-five books and an award-winning filmmaker. He has traveled the globe alongside experienced guides, naturalists, and scientists, and has spent considerable time exploring and writing about the outdoors. He has served on the board of directors for the Seattle Aquarium and works with many environmental organizations. Learn more about his work at vesperentertainment.com.

JOE ST.PIERRE has sold over two million comic books illustrating and writing for Marvel, DC, and Valiant Comics, among others. Joe also works in the fields of intellectual property design, commercial illustration, and storyboards for animation and video games. Joe's publishing company, Astronaut Ink, highlights his creator-owned properties Bold Blood, Megahurtz®, and the sold out New Zodiax. See his work at astronautink.com and popartproperties.com.